She longed to lay Vivian down on the vast sea of grass and rest naked on top of her, the warm winds stroking their bodies. She pretended that Vivian was beneath her, the hard ground acting as Vivian's muscular body, the soft grass the more tender part of her. Elizabeth breathed harder as she thought of their long night together before they had come to winter camp. Her thighs ached, her breasts ached, her lips burned. She wanted to beat her hips against the earth.

Should you lay your body down on a mattress tick abundantly stuffed with fresh prairie grass, you will sleep peacefully upon fragrant Montana feathers.

MONTANA
FEATHERS
A Novel By Penny Hayes

The Naiad Press, Inc.
1990

Printed in the United States of America
First Edition

Edited by Christine Cassidy
Cover design by Pat Tong and Bonnie Liss
    (Phoenix Graphics)
Typeset by Sandi Stancil

Library of Congress Cataloging-in-Publication Data

Hayes, Penny, 1940—
    Montana feathers / by Penny Hayes.
        p.   cm.
    ISBN 0-941483-61-4
    I. Title.
PS3558.A835M66   1990
813'.54--dc20   89-48965
                                                     CIP

To Karen

Special thanks to Nancy Doolittle

Chapter 1

Elizabeth Reynolds rammed her shovel into the sunbaked Montana soil again and again, the point of the blade scarcely making a dent in its surface. The earth she fought was sparsely covered with shriveled buffalo grass and blue-tinged sagebrush. The grass crunched beneath her feet and the sage dragged at her stockings and skirt. Dust rose from her steps and from the plunging shovel. The wind dragged dirt along its layered currents, sucking bits of grit up into the air and flinging it into her eyes. "Damn it!" she yelled and threw the shovel aside. She removed heavy

1

leather work gloves and tucked them under her arm and then rubbed her eyes clean with the back of her hand.

She had labored without pause since early morning, but now she moved with near exhaustion to a single-seated buggy. She tossed the gloves into the rear and then climbed onto the seat and collapsed in a heap. Beneath her sunbonnet, her face dripped with sweat. Rivulets formed at her temples and flowed down her cheeks and into her piercing brown eyes, stinging them with salty water. She folded back the wide brim of the bonnet and then ran her arm across her eyes, blinking and wiping sweat away. Her teeth, straight and even, showed white against her dirt-streaked face, tanned by July and August's unusually hot sun. Neatly combed this morning, her hair was now in total disarray. The bun at the base of her neck had come undone, hairpins falling out and wisps of hair sticking unpleasantly to her neck.

She stood five feet, nine inches tall, normally carrying her lean frame with regal bearing. Today, she slumped, worn out by the late morning's intense heat. Looking down at her white cotton blouse and black skirt rumpled and covered with dust, she groaned, "Lord, I'm a complete mess."

She closed her eyes, shutting out the cloudless sky, and sank against the backrest, longing for green trees and hills and grass and people crowding in on her. She recalled the night, nearly a year ago now, when she had first thought of visiting her father's sister, Polly, and her Uncle Andy Ryan on the Box R Cattle Ranch.

She had recently turned twenty-three, and she and her family had just returned home from yet another concert in New York City. By that time, Elizabeth had attended too many concerts, too many balls, and only a month after joining she had already tired of the Ladies' Tennis Club. She had known then that it wouldn't be long before she settled down forever to hearth and family, marrying Jonathan T. Stanton, and she had had a terrible fear that after marriage her life would become insufferably dull.

She longed for just one special happening that would stand out in her mind all the rest of her life, something she could think about during those times when her daily existence became too wearisome. Alone in her bedroom, she had begun to reread the letter from Aunt Polly that had arrived during the day. Sent sporadically over the years, Polly's letters always made Montana Territory sound wonderful with their vivid descriptions of cowboys and sheepherders, open spaces, clear skies, and cool starry nights. Visiting Polly and Andy for a year seemed just the opportunity she was looking for.

Elizabeth smiled when she remembered how persistently she had begged her parents to let her go. For weeks she worked on them, talking to them together, playing one against the other, soothing her father's furrowed brow with kisses, and holding her tearfully worried mother.

At the same time, she talked with Jonathan about her dream to go west before getting married. He was against the idea from the start and insisted they become betrothed at once. And afterward, he had grown even more difficult. He feared for her safety, convinced she would come to harm the very moment she stepped aboard the train. A heated argument between them failed to dissuade her. He proposed, then, that they marry as early as next spring. Elizabeth needed to stay to prepare for the wedding, he had told her, and she should be further refining herself for piano recitals and readings which would soon be held in their own home. But still, letters passed between New York and Montana. Assurances of Elizabeth's care and safety were guaranteed, and with grave reluctance, her parents had finally agreed. Jonathan nonetheless had continued to discourage her until the day she left even though she'd promised him dozens of times that she would be very careful; she would write frequently; she would telegraph the second she arrived.

Elizabeth certainly looked forward to her bridal shower and to writing wedding invitations and sharing secret little jokes with her girlfriends about married life. But Jonathan needed to understand — she first wanted to go to Montana.

Now, however, she was hot and tired and discouraged, and her tree-lined home in New York seemed much too far away.

She checked the watch hanging from a chain around her neck. It was nearly ten-thirty. She would have to return to the Box R soon. It would be just too unbearable to continue working in this heat.

On the seat beside her was a picnic basket, packed early this morning before the first rooster crowed. She pulled out a canteen and drank deeply, water splashing unheeded down her chin and onto her bosom.

Hitched to the buggy was Billy, a chestnut gelding with a white blaze streaking his face. He raised his drooping head and, looking back at Elizabeth, nickered softly. She looked at his liquid brown eyes

4

and said, "Thirsty, boy?" She climbed from the buggy and poured water from a second canteen into a bucket she had brought along for him. He smelled pleasantly musty and hot. She watched his thick, soft lips daintily sipping from the pail. When he was finished, she climbed back onto the seat.

Gazing off toward the northeast, Elizabeth wondered if she would ever get used to the endless, gently undulating earth running into the dome of unbroken sky. At least there were the mountains to the west to break up the monotony of the land.

The wind blew constantly, never stopping, Elizabeth supposed irritably, until it had circled the globe and met itself somewhere in Montana again. The strong breeze was especially bothersome today, whipping her loosened hair about her face. She brushed it aside impatiently and then rewound a fresh tight bun, painfully pulling the finer hairs at the base of her neck. She felt mean and at the same time glad that she was causing herself discomfort, frustrated that she was no further ahead on the sod house she wanted so much to build.

She had seen a number of soddies from her window while traveling aboard the Northern Pacific as the train crossed the plains of Dakota and Montana Territories and then as she'd traveled north by stagecoach from Billings to the ranch. She'd found the dwellings quaint and charming.

She had asked her aunt how sod houses were made. Polly had handed her a thin little book crudely describing sod house construction. It would be interesting to try building one, Elizabeth imagined, and not too difficult at all. Cut sod squares twelve by eighteen inches wide by two or three inches deep and then stack them bottom side up in a rectangular pattern, forming four stout walls. Rest a ridgepole across a couple of forked tree trunks driven into each end of the house and then add stick rafters and supporting material for the roof, using willow boughs or straw. Finally, lay sod strips across all of that, and there it would be, her own home — if only she could get the damn ground to give up its top layer. She glared at the pile of earth to her left. She had been at this task for three mornings now, and the measly heap of sod she had wrested from the ground lay dry and crumbly, resembling nothing about which she had read.

Her aunt and uncle had called her crazy when she'd asked if she could try building a soddy, but, surprisingly, both had agreed. Polly had even packed her first lunch for her. "We're not afraid to try new things out here, Elizabeth," she'd said, playfully pinching her niece's cheek. "Just don't make the house too big."

Andy had driven her to this spot four days ago. "You can build here, Elizabeth," he told her. "Try it if you want to. It won't hurt you, but you'll find it's easier to sit around our log house." That was true. Their house was built of thick cottonwood logs, keeping the building pleasantly cool even in the worst heat. Rectangular in design, the house was long and wide with a well-furnished kitchen positioned on the north end, a spacious living room full of comfortable chairs and a couch and large fireplace in the middle section, and two bedrooms with big feather beds on the southern end to catch the warmth of the winter sun.

There was also a big hay barn, half empty right

6

now due to this year's exceptionally dry spring and summer, and this building, too, was a wonderful place to escape the heat. A bunkhouse next to the barn was also built of logs, and although Elizabeth had never entered it, she knew it would be as cool as the ranch house. From her perch on the wagon she dwelt on each of these log oases until she made herself stop. "Go home if you find the heat this much trouble, Elizabeth," she scolded herself. But she stayed where she was.

She removed her bonnet and wiped her face dry with a lace handkerchief. Off in the distance to her left, a movement caught her attention. A hand shading her eyes, she recognized an approaching lone horseman. Uncle Andy had assured her that she would not be bothered by anyone this close to the ranch house, and she tried to remain calm as the rider drew nearer.

The stranger was almost upon her before Elizabeth realized that she was looking at a lady in trousers. She stared openly as the rider drew to a stop.

The woman sat easily in the saddle, relaxed and loose. "Howdy," she said in a husky voice. Effortlessly, she dismounted and then tied her horse to the buggy. "I'm Mrs. Blake from over on Sheephaven Ranch, the Box R's neighbor. Call me Vivian. Most everybody does."

Her wide-brimmed hat shaded grayish-blue eyes and a nose slightly too large for her darkly tanned face. Elizabeth guessed her to be thirty-five or so, with lines already deeply etched around her smiling mouth and at the corners of alert eyes. Her white teeth protruded slightly. The wind played little tricks with long blonde hair tied back with a rawhide thong. She was thin and small, her blue flannel shirt and heavy black pants hanging, loosely on her frame, revealing little evidence of her womanliness. "I wanted to welcome you," she said. "I saw your Aunt Polly a little while ago. She said you're gonna be staying on for a while."

The woman's casual manner and male attire disturbed Elizabeth, and she guardedly replied, "Yes, that's correct. It's nice to meet you."

Vivian rested an arm on the buggy. "Polly said you'd set your mind to building a soddy. My, my, my."

Elizabeth laughed lightly and relaxed. Mrs. Blake wasn't so frightening after all.

Vivian said, "It's a big job to do alone."

"I think I can manage," Elizabeth answered. "But I'm afraid I'll need help with the roof." She picked up a canteen and offered it to Vivian. "Would you care for some water? I haven't any cup."

"Don't need one." Vivian reached for the vessel and then threw back her head and drank. Wiping her chin on her sleeve, she asked, "What do you think of Montana Territory?"

"It's different," Elizabeth admitted. "And big."

"Too big, sometimes." Vivian pushed back her hat with her thumb, idly looking about the prairie.

"I thought I would be the only one with such thoughts," Elizabeth confessed.

From her back pocket Vivian pulled out a man's large red bandanna and dried her sweating face and neck. "Gets to all of us sometime or other." She jammed the bandanna back into her pocket. "There was a family come up from Tennessee three years

8

back. The prairie drove the woman crazy the very first year. She just kept saying over and over, 'Damn the wind, damn the wind.' She wasn't much good after that year, and her family hauled her back home."

"I wonder if she was given a choice about coming here," Elizabeth questioned. "It would be a hard adjustment for a woman if she were forced to live on the prairie."

The women continued talking for half an hour or so, discussing the spaciousness of Montana, the wind and dry grass, the lack of rain since springtime and its possible effects on cattle and sheep. Elizabeth was fascinated with the vast store of knowledge about ranching and animals, especially sheep, that her new acquaintance seemed to possess.

Glancing up at the sun's position, Vivian finally said, "It's getting late." She pulled out a pocket-watch, popping open the lid. Checking the time, she said, "I better be moving along. I got a ranch to run. It's been real nice to meet you. Sorry I couldn't get over to your aunt's sooner." She snapped the lid shut and then dropped the watch back into her pocket. Adjusting her hat, she moved toward her horse. "You take care. Keep your bonnet on out here. It's hot." The saddle squeaked beneath her as she mounted up and settled her rump against the cantle and pushed her spurred boots into the stirrups.

Elizabeth surmised that it must be a sheep ranch that Vivian ran. She wanted to ask her how she had gotten a sheepherder's job, whether she really was as independent as she seemed, but Vivian was in the saddle, ready to leave.

The opportunity lost, Elizabeth quickly said

9

goodbye and then stepped down from the buggy and slipped on her gloves. She felt a pressing need to begin work again before the morning was completely gone. She picked up the shovel and attacked the earth, not even waiting for Vivian to ride away.

Vivian sat motionless, watching Elizabeth. Then nodding toward the paltry heap of sod she asked, "When do you expect to finish?"

"Soon, a week. Maybe a little longer." Elizabeth continued toiling, sweating with effort.

"Polly said you were from the East. You're a Northeasterner, I'm thinkin', not a Southeasterner."

"That's right," Elizabeth grunted. She forced the shovel into the dry dirt with the heel of her shoe.

"Thought so. Southeasterners ain't so likely to try raising the dead. You ain't gonna get this thing built this year, Elizabeth. Not without help, not without rain, and for sure not without an acre of good sod. Andy's just playing a mean trick on you. He does everybody from back East. And your Aunt Polly should know better than to let him."

"I don't need rain, Vivian. I just need to keep working steadily. You know — like the hare and the tortoise. Well, I'm the tortoise. I'll get the job done and then you may be my guest for dinner." Elizabeth tried to sound optimistic.

"I don't know about any hare and tortoise," Vivian drawled. "But I'm never gonna eat here unless one of us brings a picnic basket."

"I know how to do this, Vivian," Elizabeth insisted. "I can build this house. I'm a good learner and I will do it." She *hoped* she would do it. She had never labored before, and the things that Vivian was saying made sense. But if Andy and Polly were

10

having fun with her just because she was from the East, then they were in for a big surprise. If she could talk her parents and Jonathan into letting her come to Montana, then she could certainly complete this house, and she was stubbornly determined to do it.

Vivian dismounted and walked over to Elizabeth's stack of blocks. She picked up one and began to easily break up an already crumbling corner. The dirt was instantly carried away by the wind. "If you had a decent growing season, you could sling this block onto that pile," she said. "And you could have all the sod you needed in two, maybe three days if you had some men and a couple of horses and a break plow to cut the blocks — the way you're supposed to. This ground ain't got enough grass to hold it together. It'll turn to mud come the first rain, the walls slipping to a heap, the roof leaking and caving in on you. The land is too poor right now, Elizabeth. Maybe next year."

"I've only got until next year," Elizabeth spoke strongly. "I'll never have another chance to live in my own house. I want to know what it's like to be independent. Aunt Polly talks about it all the time." The shovel came down in vicious stabs against the soil.

Vivian walked over to the buggy and leaned carelessly against its side. "What do you want to be so independent for?" she asked. "Polly ain't all that alone. Andy's there." Then she said, "Do Andy and Polly know you're actually thinking of living here?"

Elizabeth hadn't been, but now that the idea occurred to her . . .

She ignored Vivian and wrested another clump

free. Using both hands and the shovel, she was able to carefully pick up the fragile block and place it with the others.

Vivian's eyes twinkled. "You got a Montana heart in you, sure enough."

Why, she's making fun of me, thought Elizabeth. I'll show her she can't bother me. "I have a Yankee heart, Vivian," she said proudly. Thrust, push, thrust, push, went the shovel.

"Maybe so, but a Montana heart all the same. Anybody that blind stubborn has to have, even if she don't know it." Smiling, she added, "Usually, being a bit of the fool helps, too. It's how we survive out here." Vivian pushed herself off the buggy and came over to Elizabeth's side. "If you let me help, you won't have to work like a mule."

Elizabeth barely paused to look her way. "Work was never accomplished by idle hands." Her hands pained her dreadfully. Even with wearing gloves, she had blistered her palms.

"True as rain whether you're raising stock or children — or busting sod." Vivian regarded Elizabeth for a moment and then said, "Let me have the shovel." Elizabeth stopped and studied the smaller woman and then surrendered the tool to her outstretched hand. "And the gloves." Elizabeth gave these up, too. She would be glad to let Vivian dig for a while.

Instead, Vivian set the shovel and gloves aside and picked up a canteen. "Hold out your hands," she ordered, "palms up." Elizabeth obeyed and Vivian poured water over her burning, raw flesh. "Shake them dry." She stuck her finger into an axle hub and extracted a dab of grease and then smeared the lubricant into Elizabeth's hands. Elizabeth watched in fascination as Vivian tenderly treated her. Vivian's small hands were thickly calloused and darkly bronzed, their backs laced with corded veins, and their apparent great strength concealed by the woman's gentle touch.

Wiping the excess grease from her fingers against a wheel rim, Vivian said cheerfully, "There, that'll make you feel better. Best medicine there is on the range when you're far from home."

She tossed the shovel and gloves into the rear of the buggy and tied her horse to the tailgate. "Get in," she said, jumping nimbly onto the seat. She patted the space beside her. "We're going for a ride. You can live in a sod house if you're that dead set on it, and you don't have to break your back building it. For once we'll just fool your old Uncle Andy and Aunt Polly."

Faintly amused, Elizabeth climbed into the buggy, wondering at this strange woman beside her.

Chapter 2

Elizabeth and Vivian drove north for several miles before arriving at a deserted homestead. Before them stood a small sod house with a single window on the south wall and a narrow plank door facing east. Several yards away was a pump and another hundred yards beyond that a small frame barn with a corral built against one wall. Near the barn was a backhouse.

"This is it," Vivian said, jumping from the buggy. "I haven't been here in a spell." While Elizabeth trailed behind, Vivian circled the house, closely inspecting the building. She placed her hand against a wall and pushed. "Not bad. Walls are still solid as rock. Corners are still tight. Let's check inside."

Entering the low building, Elizabeth felt as though she had just stepped into her father's icehouse. The soddy's internal temperature was remarkably cool, and it was with blessed relief that momentarily she had escaped the blistering sun.

The room was sparsely furnished with a double bed, a stove, a small table, two chairs, and a dry sink. On a couple of shelves sat several hurricane lanterns beside a few pieces of silverware and metal plateware. A large cooking pot and two frying pans were stacked on the two-burner cookstove.

The soddy hadn't been occupied for some time, and the smell of dampness and mildew permeated the room. Light filtered weakly through the dusty window. The dirt floor was hard-packed and uneven. Cottonwood planking had been constructed halfway up all four walls, the remaining space covered with newspapers, cracked and brown with age. Elizabeth peered at a date: *November 17, 1879.*

Vivian observed Elizabeth's close scrutiny. "How do you like the wallpaper?" she asked. "It gives a lonely herder something to read of an evening, and it keeps the place warmer and kind of decorates it up a little. The place ain't much to look at, but you're welcome to use it. Save you time and work if you did. And there ain't no bedbugs. I always make darn sure of that because me or my hired hands still sleep here every once in a while."

Thoughtfully, Vivian ran an open palm across the top of the table. "This was mine and Tom Blake's first home. We couldn't even afford to plaster back then." With the side of her boot, she tapped the woodbox by the stove. "There's no fuel. Maybe your uncle can tote you some logs from the streams where they been washed down from the mountains. Most likely, though, somebody got them long ago. Or you can always use cats."

"Cats?"

"Grass twisted tighter than a tic. Get your aunt to show you how to make them. They're real handy. You'll be able to cook with them, and they'll keep you warm enough for a while. Later, you can buy coal from the railroad, except the cost is so high it's like buying from thieves."

Elizabeth wondered if she wasn't completely out of her mind to even consider sleeping in this primitive place, but wouldn't it be something to tell her girlfriends about *after* she got back home? She daren't write a word about it before then. If Jonathan or her parents ever found out . . .

Critically, she studied the soddy's possibilities. She need only to sweep and dust and stock up on fuel and staples. Yes, she thought she would like to try it. "I'd like to stay," she declared.

"What'll you do with your time?" Vivian asked.

"Nothing. Absolutely nothing."

Elizabeth squared her shoulders. How wonderful! She was to be on her own. And she was vastly relieved that she would no longer have to handle that shovel. She could finally admit to herself that she would probably have quit digging by tomorrow.

Vivian studied Elizabeth from beneath the brim of her hat, her head cocked a little to one side. "Can't imagine doing nothing, but you're welcome to come over and stay at my place a few days if you get tired of it here, or if you need anything. Anything at all."

Elizabeth felt a sudden closeness to this woman. She was everything Uncle Andy and Aunt Polly had claimed people of Montana to be: warm, giving, friendly. "I'll be over soon," she promised. "And thank you for your help today." She could not resist going over to the smaller woman and putting a hand on her arm. Beneath the cotton sleeve, she could feel hard muscles. She said warmly, "You are very, very kind, Vivian, and you make the prairie just a little smaller for this Easterner."

Vivian looked down at the floor and cleared her throat, letting out an embarrassed chuckle. "Haven't heard words like that for years. You got me feeling like a fool, Elizabeth."

"No need, Vivian. You *are* kind."

"Well, I'll just take your fine words as a comfort." She turned to leave. "Come on. I'll point you in the direction of the Box R. Your folks'll be looking for you, I'm thinkin'."

Outside, she described how to reach Sheephaven, her own ranch, and a few landmarks to watch for. She mounted up, gave her hat an extra downward tug, and Elizabeth a brilliant smile, and then spurred her horse northwest.

Elizabeth clucked Billy into motion, glancing back at Vivian now and then until she looked like a miniature toy before she disappeared over a small rise of land.

Elizabeth pulled Billy to a stop and sat staring at the empty horizon, wondering if Vivian had watched her driving south while she had watched Vivian riding north. She doubted it. Vivian would be too independent for such foolishness. Sheepherders, she thought, were probably loners by nature.

"Like hell you're staying in Vivian Blake's soddy," Andy Ryan growled at Elizabeth. Sitting at the kitchen table, his lanky frame towered over a cup of coffee. His bushy red eyebrows drew together and he scratched at his moustache and pursed his lips. He ran a hand through his thick mat of red hair and then, still scowling, he picked up a biscuit and smeared a huge dab of butter across its flaky top. The entire biscuit disappeared into his mouth in a single gulp.

"You and Aunt Polly said I could build a soddy, Uncle Andy," Elizabeth argued from across the table. "I found one I could live in now."

"I didn't know you wanted to *live* in it," Polly expressed herself sharply. Her blue eyes snapped as she brushed aside long strands of black hair streaked with gray. Later this morning she would braid it and wind it around her head.

Polly was thickening slightly in the middle, but muscles still rippled beneath the rolled up sleeves of her red calico dress. Gone was the slight woman Elizabeth remembered as a child, before Polly and Andy had moved to Montana from New York. Polly placed a stack of pancakes on the table and then sat down. "You said nothing about that. You don't even cook well."

"I can cook well enough to get by, Aunt Polly. I

just want to stay for a couple of nights. Maybe a week. Just for the experience."

"You, a queen in your own house," Andy said. "Your father and mother would kill you. They'd kill me, too, if I allowed it."

"Don't tell them."

"Think you're tough, do you?" Andy challenged. His green eyes bored into hers. After a long time he looked toward his wife. "What do you think, Pol? Is your niece tough?"

Polly pondered his question. Elizabeth held her breath, not daring to interrupt, hardly daring to breathe. Her aunt looked at her, studying her as intently as Andy had. Her brows were drawn into a slight scowl, and Elizabeth could barely see her blue eyes move. Polly finally answered, "Well, we lived in a soddy for nine years. I suppose she could last for a couple of nights. But you promise me, Miss Elizabeth," she said, turning on her niece with a tone leaving no doubt that she meant business, "You be back within the week."

"Oh, I will, Aunt Polly," Elizabeth promised ardently.

"Why do I feel like I just got a bad deal on a cow?" Andy gravely asked.

"I know what you mean," Polly answered.

"I'm no cow!" Elizabeth said indignantly.

"No," Andy said, "But I don't know what kind of a deal I made, either."

"Remember, Elizabeth, you promised." Polly shook a warning finger at her.

"By the end of the week, Aunt Polly."

* * * * *

19

Polly insisted on going with Elizabeth to help clean the soddy. "You're not going to sleep in a damn dirt building without it's being hoed out from top to bottom first," she said grumpily. "If your parents ever find out Andy and I let you stay here all alone, I can at least tell them you were properly installed. You keep that door closed, you hear? We don't have locks out here, but folks'll respect a closed door on an occupied building."

They spent two days cleaning out cobwebs, dusting every item in the place, sweeping the floor a dozen times, washing the window and tableware, and stuffing the woodbox with the cats that Polly taught Elizabeth to make. The first day, Polly brought along fresh blankets and sheets and a feather mattress, saying, "I don't care if Vivian Blake claims she has no bedbugs in here. It's best to be sure." She removed the old tick from the bed and walked all the way to the barn before emptying it of stale and crumpling buffalo grass.

The women did not stop working until the soddy met with Polly's complete satisfaction. Elizabeth didn't realize there was so much to do. At home, servants would have taken care of all this drudgery. Here, she had taken up a dust cloth for the first time in her life and found she rather enjoyed tidying up.

The following afternoon she and Polly had loaded the buggy with ample supplies and tonight Elizabeth would sleep in the soddy. There wouldn't be another living soul within miles of her. She would find out how great was the freedom of being alone.

By ginger, she was ready to leave!

Andy had purposely come in early from the range

to see her off. He and Polly followed her out of the house. "You remember to keep your door shut, like I told you," Polly said. "There're all kinds of creatures roaming around."

"I will, Aunt Polly." Elizabeth took a deep breath, looking at them both and said, "Well."

"I expect you'll do fine, Elizabeth," her uncle assured her. "You're a lot like your Aunt Polly." He hugged Elizabeth and shushed his wife when she started to remind her niece once again to return on time.

"What will you do out there all alone?" Polly asked. Nervously, she fiddled with her apron while Andy made a final check on Elizabeth's supplies and Billy's straps, making sure she had harnessed him correctly.

"I'll sleep late each morning and drink coffee until I burst," she answered. "And just walk and walk until I get tired. At night, I'm going to sit by the fire and doze, and when I read, I'm going to dally over each word before going on to the next."

"You could do all that right here," Polly pronounced.

"You worry too much, Aunt Polly."

She gave her aunt and uncle a hug and then climbed into the buggy. They called goodbyes to one another, waving long after it was practical. Finally, Elizabeth turned forward and breathed deeply of the restless prairie wind.

Arriving late in the day, she hurried to unload the buggy, carrying in the last of the drygoods, a large slab of smoked bacon, potatoes, beans, onions, herbs, spices, and coffee. She laughed out loud at the pile of supplies overloading the table and bed. Polly was determined that Elizabeth would not go hungry for the next few days.

Elizabeth drove into the barn and unhitched Billy. She turned him into the corral and then stopped at the backhouse. It, too, had been cleaned out and wood ashes from the ranch had been thrown down into both holes. An old Sears, Roebuck catalog had been put inside for use.

She had just exited when she heard the unmistakable sound of a rattle not a yard's distance from her foot. She didn't need to live in Montana to recognize the warning. Glancing down cautiously, she saw the long serpent — sleek, coiled, ready. She became lightheaded, thinking she might faint. If she did, she would be bitten. She fought her fear and closed her eyes, concentrating on remaining motionless while her head swam and cold sweat broke out on her forehead. She remembered reading somewhere that an animal could smell fear, and she tried to steady herself so that the snake would not know how terrified she was. Gradually her head cleared, and she heard again the dreaded rattle. Still she did not move nor open her eyes, taking only shallow breaths. Minutes passed before she allowed herself the slightest motion to check the snake's position. Tears of relief filled her eyes when she saw that it had moved off. It was still nearby, but even if it struck, it was now out of her range. Slowly, she inched away from the backhouse in case its small base of rocks concealed more of the venomous creatures.

She walked woodenly to the house, weak-kneed

and trembling from head to foot. She glanced back frequently, feeling as if the horrible viper was slithering after her. She backed through the open door, pulling it tight behind her, and then closed her eyes and rested her forehead against the rough wood, feeling safe at last.

"Howdy."

The unexpected male voice turned her to stone. Too late, she remembered Polly's frequent warnings about keeping the door closed. Suddenly dizzy, Elizabeth moaned slightly and then felt strong arms catch her and carry her to the bed.

"Don't be afraid, Missy," the burred voice spoke. "I'm Mrs. Blake's herder."

She looked up uncomprehendingly, her eyes not quite focused. The man's hands were still on her shoulders. Terrorized, she waited for the worst to happen.

"You'll be all right, Missy. Mrs. Blake sent me to see if you were here, if the herd worked over this way."

She could see him clearly now. He was a small sinewy man with eyes as black as coal. His graying hair hung to his shoulders. He smiled, showing tobacco-stained teeth in a face creased with age and blackened from years beneath the sun. He wore a checkered shirt, opened at the throat, and pants worn thin at the knees. His boots were dusty and badly scratched. "I'm Henry Hawk."

The loud barking of a dog drew their attention to the door. "There's a snake . . . a rattler . . ." Elizabeth managed to say.

Vicious snarls sent Henry on the run to the

backhouse. With fear bordering on panic, Elizabeth forced herself to get up and follow him, but she went only as far as the end of the soddy wall.

She watched Henry call off a big black and white dog barking and clawing frantically at the backhouse foundation. The sheepherder drew a gun from inside his shirt and fired once. The crack of the pistol made Elizabeth jump. She saw the snake's head splatter against the ground.

Henry reached down and withdrew the snake from the rocks and then drew a knife from a boot sheath and unceremoniously severed the rattle from the snake's tail. With the toe of his boot, he lifted the five-foot rattler and kicked it out onto the prairie. "Get'm, Samson."

At Henry's wave, the dog ran after the snake, grabbing it in the middle. Growling with sounds of near madness, the dog viciously shook the serpent, snapping its back before releasing it. He sniffed at the mutilated body and then wriggling and panting, trotted over to his master's side.

"Good boy, Samson." Henry reached down and patted the dog.

Samson followed Henry and Elizabeth to the soddy door. "Sit, Samson," Henry commanded. Obediently, the dog rested on his haunches.

Inside, Henry said, "Here, ma'am," and offered the six-inch rattle to Elizabeth. Shuddering inwardly, she accepted his ghastly gift, barely noticing his pleased look. She dropped the rattle on the floor beside the dry sink. As soon as Henry Hawk left, she would bury it.

At the sink, Elizabeth repeatedly scrubbed her

24

hands, thinking she would never be able to wash the feel of the rattle from her fingers. Deciding that she was behaving foolishly in front of Henry, she reluctantly dried her hands and draped the towel over the back of a chair. "I want to thank you for destroying the snake."

He waved her words away as he sat at the table, looking expectantly at her. To fill the awkward silence she asked, "Would you like some coffee?"

"And grub."

She flushed with embarrassment that she hadn't thought right away to offer him something to eat. "I'll prepare something immediately," she said and hastened to stuff some cats into the stove. Hereafter, she would certainly remember.

She lighted the cats, and smoke began to fill the cabin. She struggled with the flames, unwilling to profess her ignorance of fire-building to Henry. The fire went out twice, and even with the soddy door wide open the room became unbearably smoky.

She was in tears, not from the smoke, but from her ineptitude. She had been at the soddy not quite an hour, but in that time she couldn't remember a single thing she had done right or that she felt good about.

Wordlessly, Henry went to the stove and opened the damper, allowing the smoke to escape up the pipe and fresh air to feed the fire through the door. Putting a few more cats into the belly, he closed the door and then sat again. He said, "Open and close the damper as much as you need to feed your flame."

By the time most of the smoke had cleared out, Elizabeth had filled Henry's plate with fried potatoes and bacon. She was glad now that she had taken the time to have her family's cook teach her some basics in cooking.

Years of training had taught Elizabeth to bow her head before meals. Henry, head of the table by virtue of being the only man present, would, of course, say grace. But Henry had already begun digging into his meal. Elizabeth picked up her fork and began eating, too.

When he was finished, Henry donned his brimmed hat and thanked her, then quietly left with Samson trailing behind. The herder stepped briskly along, with Elizabeth wondering how he had managed walking in the day's earlier heat. She watched after him until he disappeared over a small hill.

The sweep of a large hawk circling above caught her eye. Suddenly, it dove at an incredible speed, striking a few yards from the barn. There was a scream, and the bird flew skyward, a large rabbit gripped in its talons. The hawk's act chilled Elizabeth. Moments before she had been admiring the beauty of the graceful creature. Now she just wished it gone.

Darkness closed in on the sod house, and Elizabeth went in to get the rattle. After burying it out back of the soddy, she checked to see that she had enough cats for the evening and then firmly closed the door against the encroaching night.

Elizabeth awoke in the night, needing to use the chamberpot. As she sat with her nightgown bunched up around her waist so that it would not touch the floor, something skittered across her bare feet. She shrieked in fear, instinctively drawing in her feet tight against the pot. She jumped up, her hands flailing wildly at the surrounding space. "Dear God," she fervently prayed. "Please don't let me touch anything alive."

She leaped into bed and lighted a lantern that she had placed on a chair beside her bed. With shaking hands, she passed the lantern back and forth, seeing nothing out of the ordinary. Still jittery over her earlier scare, she did not dare get out of bed again, although she knew that if a snake wanted to crawl into the bed with her, it could.

She set down the lantern, still burning, and sat with her knees drawn and the covers pulled tightly around her until the break of day. She breathed a grateful sigh of relief as dawn dusted her window with hues of gray, breaking up the long night's blackness. She heard a noise to her left and saw two shadowy images scamper across the table. She heard a squeak and flung a shoe at the table, screeching, "Get out!" Tiny field mice scampered onto the floor, escaping through a hole in the wall. Sick to her stomach, she rested her head against her knees and questioned the toughness Uncle Andy seemed to believe she possessed.

As soon as it was light enough, she dressed, ate, and then went to harness Billy, planning to drive to the ranch for the day. She decided it was better to be there than sitting inside the soddy all day — afraid. One's own home was a brave thing to have. She would ask Aunt Polly how she handled things whenever she was alone.

Elizabeth was halfway there when she halted and

turned back. She would not return to her aunt's after all. Admit she had been afraid after a single night's stay in the soddy? Aunt Polly would have her packed and out of there this morning, and Uncle Andy would laugh at her. And what of Vivian Blake? She couldn't possibly have Vivian learn that she hadn't even lasted twenty-four hours. That woman had never once suggested she wouldn't make it. No, she must go back and stay to face whatever real or imaginary things were there.

She staked Billy near the barn. Come mid-morning, she would put him inside. By then the sun would be too hot for man or beast.

She entered the house, thinking she would clean it thoroughly, but the small dwelling had already been cleaned as much as possible. She recalled the walking and reading and the drinking of coffee that she had planned to do, but she didn't feel like doing any of these things.

She stepped back outside and looked around at her lonely surroundings. Above her, clouds billowed like giant puffballs against a sky of china-blue. The buffalo grass, scorched by the sun, was brown as a walnut. A rabbit hopped into view near the corral and then was gone.

Sighing deeply, she went inside to while away a quiet day.

Chapter 3

Elizabeth harnessed Billy twice more over the next two days, starting out once for the Box R and once toward Vivian's, only to turn back each time, displeased with herself for running to them — for that's what it amounted to. She thought she should be able to face *two* days alone by herself. At least she hadn't experienced any additional bad frights other than the mice insisting upon coming in each night.

She had already consumed all the reading material she had brought with her, including a novel, a couple of magazines, a small cookbook given to her by Polly, and even the newspapers on the walls. She read, too, from a small leather-bound Bible, a going-away gift from her parents, reading only the Apostles and letters of John, avoiding the Old Testament as too bloody, Revelations as too disquieting, and Paul as too strict for her way of thinking.

She had also blocked several new mouse holes, curried Billy each morning, made cats, and afterward, her reading done, struggled to fill the rest of her days. But today she needed to talk to someone. Her prairie home had become just too vast for her, and on the third morning she gave up and went back to the Box R two days sooner than she had planned.

"Aunt Polly, I'm home," she called out.

Polly came running out of the house. "Got lonesome, huh?" She held her arms open, waiting for Elizabeth to come down off the buggy. "I knew you'd be back long before the week was out. What'd you do there? You aren't a girl who can live like that, Elizabeth. You're not used to it. I told your uncle that a hundred times since you left. You need care and attention. That's what I needed when I was your age, and that's what you need."

"Good morning, Aunt Polly," Elizabeth managed to squeeze in between her aunt's disturbing torrent of words.

"Come on down from there, girl, and come inside where it's cool. I've got tea and lemonade made up. I knew you'd give in. I'm so glad you did."

Admittedly, Elizabeth had been lonesome. But did she really need all that care that Polly was babbling about? Did Uncle Andy think that way about her, too? Did others? She wouldn't stand for it! Rashly, she said, "That's not why I'm here, Aunt Polly. Last week, Mrs. Blake invited me to visit Sheephaven for a few days, and I accepted. I plan to go there tomorrow. I'm only here to tell you that." At least Vivian Blake didn't think she was an invalid.

"You don't mean it!" Polly declared. "Well, I'll just talk to your uncle about this. We promised your parents you would be well taken care of. I don't see that your going over there all alone is taking care of you at all." In a huff, she went back into the house, leaving Elizabeth to follow after her.

That evening over supper, Polly surprised Elizabeth by saying, "You're right, dear. You should visit Vivian Blake if that's what you want to do."

"Aunt Polly!" Her aunt hadn't said a word all day about her going. What had changed her mind?

Slowly, Andy lowered his cup. "You sure about this, Pol?"

"I've been thinking about something today, Andy," she said. "You remember the time I rode that piebald mare forty miles to get you a doctor when you took sick? That was only a year after we got here, Elizabeth. Lord, I was terrified."

"You never wrote Father about that, Aunt Polly," Elizabeth said. "Why are you telling me?"

"Your father wouldn't have been pleased — and you are a Reynolds. Besides, Sheephaven's only a fifteen-mile trip — and Andy will drive part of the

31

way for you. He has to go out that way, and he can take his horse right along with him. My goodness, you should be all right with Vivian Blake."

Andy looked at his niece. "I guess that's right, Elizabeth."

She felt a cold reluctance on his part. It wasn't that he didn't want her to go. Something else was bothering him. At least he wasn't stopping her. "Then I'll leave early in the morning," she told them.

He asked, "How long do you expect to stay at Sheephaven?"

"A few days. And remember, I came back early this time, just as I promised. I will do so again."

That night in bed, Elizabeth thought, I wouldn't leave but for your words this morning, Aunt Polly. Your agreeing that I may go does not wipe them out. I will not — for a second — have anyone consider me an incompetent woman.

The following morning, Elizabeth followed Vivian's landmarks to Sheephaven. She drew the buggy up to the door of a large cottonwood log house with windows front and back and a large plank door centered midway in the building. A pump stood near the door and, a hundred yards away, a small henhouse abutted a barn and large corral. Near the barn was a bunkhouse. Behind it, a windmill creaked, its vanes spinning in the wind, its rusty sounds mixing with the loud clucking of irate chickens.

A tall, heavy man came out of the house carrying a sack of grain slung across a broad shoulder. He was whiskered and bronzed, and his blue eyes crinkled with merriment. A wide-brimmed hat, pushed far back on his head, partially concealed a balding scalp. "Howdy," he said, and smiled. Effortlessly, he threw the sack into the rear of a miniature covered wagon.

"Good morning," Elizabeth replied. "I'm looking for Vivian Blake." She flipped back the brim of her sunbonnet, climbed from the buggy, and stood shaking her blue dress free of wrinkles.

"I'm right here," Vivian said, grinning widely. She came from the direction of the henhouse, carrying a small bucket of eggs. She wore men's clothing, and again Elizabeth was jarred to look upon a woman in pants.

"I hope I'm not interrupting anything," Elizabeth said.

"I thought you'd show up before this," Vivian answered heartily. "Al, meet Elizabeth Reynolds. Elizabeth, Al Sterling. He runs sheep with me. Take these eggs inside, Al. Pack them in the bag of oats. Don't forget that slab bacon." She turned to Elizabeth. "How're you making out?"

Elizabeth answered enthusiastically, "Oh, fine, just fine. Plenty to do. I write dozens of letters home. I go driving each morning before it gets too hot. I've made a few improvements on the soddy." She felt no need to mention that Jonathan would be telegraphing her if she didn't write daily or why she had taken those drives or that the improvements were plugged mouse holes.

Vivian looked skeptically at her and then invited her inside. "I've got some lemon crystals," she said. "I'll make us some lemonade. Take a look around if you like."

The house was divided into a kitchen and

33

bedroom to the left and a large parlor to the right. A couple of pictures hung on walls of blue and gray flowered wallpaper. In the kitchen, now cluttered with supplies Al was steadily moving out, was an oven and stove. Nearby was a round oak table surrounded by four spindle-backed chairs. Dishes sat on a fine china cabinet, pots and pans hung from the ceiling. An oak dresser and mirror stood in the bedroom, alongside a double bed covered with two fat pillows and a patchwork quilt. Next to the door was a small closet. The parlor held a horsehair couch and two stuffed chairs; hurricane lanterns sat on stands by the couch and chairs. Between the bedroom and parlor wall was a large fireplace built to simultaneously serve both rooms.

"You're seeing the place at its best, except for the kitchen," Vivian said. "Doesn't look this good most of the time." She handed Elizabeth a sweating glass of lemonade. "Here you are. Ice cold water from the pump."

Elizabeth removed her bonnet and then sat at the table and drank deeply, the swirling crystals tasting wonderfully tangy.

Vivian poured her another. "Henry said you make fine vittles. He said you're mighty brave, too."

"I question that." Elizabeth chuckled. "But thank you for sending him to check on me. I'm glad he came along when he did."

"How long did you stay at the soddy?" Vivian asked. She rinsed their glasses at the sink and then set them aside to drain.

"I was there three days. Aunt Polly insisted I return early. I think I like being alone." Why, she wondered, did she say that? She had hated every minute there.

"All finished, Vivian." Al's bass voice filled the kitchen.

"Be right there. I have to go, Elizabeth. I'll be back in a few days. Al will be here if you need anything."

Vivian was leaving? Elizabeth had expected to spend a couple of nights here. Incredulously, she asked, "Do you camp out on the range?"

"All the time," Vivian answered. She lifted her hat off a hook by the door and turned at the threshold, waiting for Elizabeth.

Elizabeth knew she should rise and leave. If only Aunt Polly hadn't said all those things. But she wasn't going to go back to the Box R, looking like a lonely, simpering child. She would stay at the soddy for a couple of days first, and then she would return. But she didn't *want* to return — not to the Box R, *nor* the soddy. She clung to Vivian through lying words. "I won't be needing anything. I'm perfectly fine."

Vivian stared intently at her, and Elizabeth looked away. "How would you like to come along?" she suggested.

"Oh, no, I'm so busy, I don't see how I could."

"You ain't got one damn thing to do at that soddy that I know of," Vivian challenged. "In fact, you made it a point to mention you weren't going to do anything, as I recollect."

Elizabeth remembered her vow to laziness. "So I did. It hasn't been like that, however. I have been busy."

35

"Reading the walls, I'm thinkin'. Come on with me. You'll enjoy the ride. You want to wear pants?"

"Absolutely not," Elizabeth flatly stated. "My dress will do just fine."

"Just get you some boots out of the bedroom closet, then. There's something in there that'll fit. If you brought an overnight bag, throw it in the wagon. Otherwise I'll give you some clothes. Al can take care of your horse while you're gone. You'll be out a week. Sorry I can't wait and leave with you early tomorrow morning, so that you didn't have to ride in this heat, but I have to get supplies to Henry. I'll find you a bigger sunbonnet. That'll help."

Elizabeth looked across the prairie shimmering with heat. Aunt Polly would never agree with what she was about to do. Elizabeth was sure of it.

Vivian drove the two-horse team with practiced ease. "This is Mike and Skip," she said, pointing toward each horse.

Sitting beside her on the narrow wagon seat, Elizabeth looked at the tightly packed food and supplies in back. A tiny dry sink and two narrow slabs of wood that served as beds had been built on each side, with compact storage areas underneath. A small cook stove sat near the back, its pipe extending up through the canvas top.

"Fella named Jim Candlish down in Rawlins, Wyoming makes these sheep wagons," Vivian said. "I ordered this one soon as I heard about him. When it's raining, these little buggies sure beat sleeping on the ground. I can handle only so much camping before I get a hankering for home, and the comforts of this wagon are as close as I can get."

An extra horse, tied to the rear of the wagon, trailed behind. Even with walking slowly, the animals frothed with sweat. The air was still for a moment, and Elizabeth found it difficult to breathe. "I don't think I've ever known hotter weather." She removed her bonnet and mopped her face with a handkerchief.

"You get used to it after a while but I do get to longing for the cool hills of Kentucky on days like this," Vivian remarked. "But then I remember all the people crowding in on me the last time I went back to visit my family. Now Montana's crowded. Didn't used to be. You could drive a day — two days — and never see another living soul. Folks been talking statehood for quite awhile now. Couple of years and it'll happen. You wait and see. Too many people."

"Do you like solitude that much?" Elizabeth asked.

"Usually. Still, one person can fill out the life of another. Kind of like adding a finishing touch. After a while, a person alone just rattles around like a stone in an empty bucket. But I ain't in no hurry to fill the bucket again." She laughed and heartily slapped Elizabeth on the knee, surprising her with her familiarity.

"And your husband, Vivian. Where is he?"

"Tom's buried over in the west section. He was helping a neighbor dig a well and it caved in on him. We got him out in time, but he had too many places crushed up inside him."

"I'm sorry."

"No need. It's been five years."

The land rose and fell in gentle waves as the

wagon moved slowly eastward. Vivian pointed off to their right. "A herd of sheep was rim-rocked right over that ridge in '82. Damn sneaking gunnysackers did it. Fine bunch of cowards, their faces all covered up with sacks. You get five or six sheep moving, the rest will follow. Pretty soon the whole blamed herd's on the move. Well, over they went. Every blessed one."

"Did you ever lose a herd that way?" Elizabeth asked.

"Nope, we weren't near this section then. We came after the cattlemen and sheepherders got all done shooting at each other. Tom swore he'd shoot dead the first cattleman that set foot near his herd — even if the shot stampeded the whole bunch and cost him the lot of them. Word got around he'd taken a pop or two at a couple of cowboys. I never knew him to shoot at anybody. Maybe he started the rumor himself. If he did, it worked."

Vivian clucked to the horses that had nearly stopped moving. "Getup, Mike, getup Skip." Gently, she encouraged them forward.

"Cattlemen don't like sheep coming onto their range. The sheep eat the grass down to nubs. Then their hooves cut up the roots so bad, grass ain't likely to grow till next year's rains. That's why you gotta keep them moving from place to place. Tom got together with the cattlemen right after we got here and they all decided on a deadline. Nobody crosses it. Most ranchers are beginning to run bobwire now, so a deadline ain't so necessary anymore. Me, I just stay east and avoid everybody."

"There's so much to know," Elizabeth said. "How did you learn?"

"Just did. Made mistakes, learned from them."

Late in the afternoon the sound of bleating and blatting floated toward them. At the next rise, Elizabeth saw the massive herd. There were at least four thousand of them; fat, fleeced sheep with colors running from white to tan to black. Dust rose above their backs and was whisked away by the wind. Four black and white dogs moved continuously at a rapid pace, circling the herd, quickly squatting down on haunches, only to be up and moving again as soon as a sheep strayed. From the far side of the herd Henry whistled and waved, sending a dog to the left to tighten the flock. Elizabeth recognized Samson and marveled at the dog's self-assuredness and quickness and understanding of what was expected of him.

Awed by the sight before her, Elizabeth asked, "How can just one person keep track of all these sheep?"

Vivian explained. "There's usually two people here. Al, Henry, and me rotate around, so nobody has to stay out for too many weeks at a time. Al's in now, and I'm out. Some herders go out on the range and don't see anybody for six or eight months. I couldn't stand that."

Elizabeth had noticed a heavy, musky odor which became stronger and more pungent as they drew nearer the noisy herd. By the time Vivian stopped the wagon, Elizabeth found breathing through her nose impossible. She climbed from the wagon, hating the smell and wishing the wind were blowing in the opposite direction.

Vivian handed the reins to Elizabeth. "Unhitch the horses and stake them to that bush there. Give them plenty of lead rope so they can graze. You can

39

water them over at that waterhole, yonder. I'll show you how to hobble them later." Without further explanation, she jumped from the wagon and headed toward Henry, leaving Elizabeth to wonder how to unharness the big team and resenting Vivian's nonchalant attitude. No one had ever ordered her about before.

She climbed from the seat and began to unbuckle straps, not knowing if they were the correct buckles to release or not. She pulled off the horses' collars, piling their heavy leather tack in a tangled heap on the ground before carelessly kicking it all beneath the wagon. She watered the thirsty animals and then led them to the bush and tied them there.

The more she thought about Vivian's request — no, *command* was a better word — the more indignant she became. "I didn't come here to work," she muttered as she walked back to the wagon. She lowered the tailgate and plunked down on it. She sighed discontentedly and looked around at her surroundings, already bored with nothing to do.

A half hour later, Vivian and Henry returned together. Vivian asked, "Got chow going?"

"No," Elizabeth answered. It hadn't occurred to her that she was expected to cook.

"Everything you need is right in the wagon," Vivian told her. "But cook outdoors. It'll be cooler."

Elizabeth supposed she was willing enough to try. She liked to cook. But what was she to use as fuel on this woodless prairie? "Should I make cats?" she asked.

From the wagon Henry tossed an old grain bag to the ground. "Here, Missy, use these," he said, and joined Vivian, who had moved off and was relaxing on the ground.

Piqued that they paid her no more attention than that, Elizabeth turned her back on the sheepherders and opened the bag. The odor of cow manure floated up to her. "Ugh,"she muttered and then turned her head to see if she had been heard, but no one heeded her.

Gingerly, she reached in and picked out a chunk of dried manure. "Lordy, how am I going to do this?" she whispered. "I should never have agreed to cook."

It took almost an hour, and half the bag of chips, to prepare the meal. The wind blew her fire out three times. Pots, pans, and food supplies had been tightly packed, and often she had had to move two or three items to reach what she needed. The bag of preroasted coffee beans, buried as deep as everything else, had been purchased in Billings a month ago. The coffee was from Java, Vivian had said — the best that money could buy. Out on the plains at night, she'd told Elizabeth, nothing beat a good hot cup of high-toned coffee. Elizabeth opened the bag savoring the rich aroma and ground the beans using a small hand-held coffee mill. At least she enjoyed *that* chore.

With sweat streaming down her face she was finally able to say, "Come and get it."

The herders strolled over and Vivian said, "Smells good, Elizabeth." She began filling her plate, loading it down heavily with hominy and thick slices of bacon and a large slab of johnnycake. "I'll take coffee, too." She held out an empty cup and waited for Elizabeth to fill it. Elizabeth did, beginning to question just why Vivian had asked her to come along. Henry, too, expectantly held out his cup and plate, and she gave him at least as much food as Vivian had taken. Finally it was her turn. She helped herself to only half the amount of food as had the others, yet the food was gone. She could easily have eaten more, but she had not cooked enough. Well, it would just have to do.

"Why don't you bake more cake, Elizabeth?" Vivian asked, her plate nearly empty. "It won't take but a minute to whip it up."

"Uhh," Henry grunted. "More grits, too." He dug into the last of his meal.

"You want me to cook again?" Elizabeth wasn't sure Vivian was serious.

"Just take you a minute," Vivian said, looking straight at her. The woman was dead serious, Elizabeth realized.

Fighting her rapidly rising anger, Elizabeth clamped her jaw so that she wouldn't say something rash. It would only take Vivian a minute to cook, too — in fact, probably only half a minute. But it didn't look like she was going to move. If it were at all possible, returning to her lonely soddy right now struck Elizabeth as a splendid idea.

It took her almost as long to cook this time as last, but she got through the tedious chore, and again sat down to complete her meal.

Having finished a second helping of hominy and johnnycake, Henry stood and patted his belly. "Good, Missy."

At least there was a kind word from him, Elizabeth thought.

He dusted his hat against his leg. "Better be moving."

"Be seeing you," Vivian said.

"Yep." He walked over to the extra horse and jerked its rein free of the bush. He mounted bareback and rode over to Elizabeth. "Nice seeing you, Missy," he said and turned west. In five minutes, he was a shadow on the horizon.

"Where's he going?" Elizabeth asked. Was he leaving Vivian and her all alone out here? This was no place for lone women.

"He's going home," Vivian casually answered. "He'll be back in a week to join me."

"But what about the sheep?" Elizabeth asked. "There's just you now — and four dogs."

Unconcerned, Vivian said, "That's enough with you here, too."

"Me? What about me? I don't even know what I'm doing."

Vivian stood and stretched. "You're doing fine, Elizabeth, just fine. That's why I sent Henry home." She let out a piercing whistle and waved a dog toward some strays to the left. A loud "hiya" completed the signal, and she began to head in that direction. Over her shoulder she called out, "I'll be back by dark. Have some coffee ready, will you?"

Her fists jammed against her hips, Elizabeth sputtered, "Of all the unmitigated gall. You could have at least carried your dish over to the tailgate!" Her words were useless. Vivian was already out of earshot.

She slopped hot water into a pan and wrathfully began to scrub and stack dishes. Soapy water splashed onto the tailgate and her dress. She didn't care if she broke something. The dishtowel snapped and dishes flew into their assigned places. She pitched the rinse water onto the ground and then hung the pan on the tailgate. Striding rapidly around the wagon and horses and then further out onto the prairie, she fought to bring her temper under control. She was *never* out of control. By the time she needed to start the fire again she had calmed down considerably, until, cringing, she reached into the grain bag for a chip. She was sorry she had ever agreed to visit Vivian Blake.

Vivian showed Elizabeth how to hobble the horses and then by lantern light she prepared their beds. She threw a buffalo robe across each cot. "It ain't gonna be like sleeping on Montana feathers, but it'll do."

"What're Montana feathers?" Elizabeth asked grumpily. When Vivian had come in, she had angered Elizabeth all over again. Vivian shouldn't have held out her coffee cup that way. She should have poured her own coffee.

Vivian rolled two shirts and put one at the head of each bed. "Montana feathers are mattress ticks stuffed with fresh hay or grass. They smell good and feel great. But you'll be glad enough you're in this buffalo robe about midnight. Nights are getting cold."

"I haven't seen any buffalo around." Elizabeth glanced anxiously into the encroaching darkness. With her luck, there was probably one about to charge her right now.

"They're all gone. Been gone for a decade."

Vivian stepped out of the wagon while Elizabeth changed into her flannel nightgown. She got into bed and drew the robe around her. Although the covering was warm enough, it seemed to weigh tons, anchoring her to the bed. She tossed and turned for a minute, finding that there was no way to get comfortable. She couldn't bear to think that she would be sleeping this way for a whole week.

Vivian climbed into the wagon and sat on the edge of her bed. With a grunt, she pulled off her boots, dropping them carelessly to the floor. Still fully clothed, she slid beneath the covers and then reached up and turned out the light, plunging the wagon into an inky blackness. Elizabeth heard her sigh deeply and then say, "G'night, Elizabeth." By her breathing, Elizabeth guessed that she had already fallen asleep.

For an hour Elizabeth lay staring into the night, her mind a turmoil of thoughts. When Vivian had asked her along, Elizabeth hadn't considered the primitive conditions under which she would be living. She had certainly never anticipated becoming one of the hands. No doubt if Henry were still here he would work the herd and Vivian would take care of the horses and the cooking for all three of them.

Elizabeth tried to ignore Vivian's unpleasant sounds as the woman lay moaning in her sleep. During the past hour her breathing had changed. In just the last five minutes or so she had apparently begun dreaming, groaning even more, as if in intense pain. Elizabeth listened to her sounds until she could stand it no longer. She slipped on her boots and left the wagon.

The western sky, ablaze with stars, seemed incredibly near. Childlike, Elizabeth reached up to touch one. She shivered from the cold night air and wrapped her arms tightly around herself. Then she

45

strolled a short distance away from the wagon. Silvery moonlight made seeing easy, and out of instinct she glanced around before lifting her nightgown to be sure no one was watching. She felt much better when she could start back to the wagon.

Unexpectedly, there came a growl nearby, low and threatening. Elizabeth stopped dead in her tracks, not daring to move another step. Her experience with the rattler tore through her mind. It just wasn't safe to walk *anywhere* on the prairie. The growl came again, louder this time — and closer. The distance to the wagon was at least ten yards. Even if she ran as fast as she could, she would never make it. On their trip out, Vivian had told her that there were foxes here, and coyotes and antelopes — and mountain lions. She envisioned the cat hamstringing her and then tearing her neck to shreds. She could already feel its long sharp fangs sinking into her flesh.

Frozen with fear, she never heard the animal come up to her until a cold, wet nosed touched her forearm. She let out a shriek, certain that she had seen her last sunset. Two paws landed heavily against her chest, and a great wet tongue lapped her chin. Aghast, she stared down into a large hairy face and then gasped loudly with relief. "Dog — not . . . cat! Oh! A wonderful, wonderful sheepdog. It's you, isn't it, Samson?" The dog barked, making her leap, and she looked frantically toward the shadowy herd bedded down for the night. Earlier today Vivian had told her that sheep would bolt in the night over unexpected sounds. She wondered why they hadn't already, but, thank goodness, they remained stationary.

She pushed Samson aside. "Don't do that again,

Samson," she scolded softly and watched him fade into the night. After an age, her heart calmed down.

She heard another moan from the wagon and decided that she must wake Vivian from her nightmare after all.

"Vivian,"she said as she entered the wagon. She shook the woman slightly. "Vivian, you're dreaming."

"Get me some whiskey," Vivian said. "There in the drawer beneath your bed."

"You're dreaming, Vivian."

"I'm sick. Get me some whiskey."

Vivian, sick? But why hadn't she said something before this?

Elizabeth lit a lamp and dug out the whiskey and then held a cup to Vivian's lips.

"Where don't you feel good?" Elizabeth asked.

"My stomach. It's happened before, but I'll be all right by morning." Vivian held her hand pressed against her right side and drank again, more deeply this time. Soon she seemed to calm down and then, finally, to sleep.

Vivian's shirt was soaked with sweat. She was obviously running a fever. Elizabeth dipped her handkerchief into a water bucket and then wiped Vivian's forehead. The woman didn't move as Elizabeth repeatedly cooled her face. Elizabeth held her watch to the light. It was now eleven PM. She would stay up and keep her eye on Vivian. She didn't know what else she could do. The hours until daylight seemed incredibly long.

* * * * *

At first light, Vivian rolled spryly out of bed. "Coffee ready?"

"Are you all right?" Elizabeth asked. "You . . ."

Impatiently, Vivian interrupted. "Never mind that. How about that coffee?"

"In a minute. What about how you feel?"

"I'm fine. Don't worry about me. I hate a complainer."

If Vivian didn't want to discuss how sick she had been, then Elizabeth wouldn't. But she was deeply concerned, nevertheless. She waited for Vivian to leave the wagon before getting dressed. And it looked like she would be cooking all week. With resignation, she accepted her role and picked up the eggs as she left the wagon.

Vivian drank a dipperful of water and then said, "I thought I heard a dog bark in the night."

"I disturbed Samson," Elizabeth explained.

Vivian looked uneasily at her. "Those damn sheep like to take off at night now and then, or start eating in the middle of the night. It can be annoying." She hung up the dipper and turned to leave. "I'll be back in half an hour or so."

Elizabeth watched the herd begin to rise. The air filled with their noises and their obnoxious smell became stronger as they moved about.

She cooked outside again, and had coffee boiling and bacon and eggs frying in a pan in less time than it took Vivian to return. She felt a tiny sense of accomplishment at having prepared breakfast so fast. She was much better this morning at getting the fire going and successfully keeping it burning. This time she had simply dumped the chips into a pile instead of handling them one by one. Why hadn't she done

48

that yesterday, she wondered. It made so much more sense.

A short time later, Vivian came in. Elizabeth filled a plate, then sat on a packing box in the shade of the wagon and began to eat. Vivian watched her for a couple of seconds and then said, "Guess I'll eat now."

"Go ahead," Elizabeth replied. "The bacon's better today than it was yesterday."

"I thought you'd fill my plate for me."

"I'll cook, but I'm not waiting on you anymore." Elizabeth was going to get this settled now.

Vivian smiled and reached for an empty plate.

"What's so funny?" Elizabeth asked.

"Those are the same words I said to Al and Henry the first time I cooked for the three of us."

"You can fill your own coffee cup, too, *and* take your dish over to the tailgate."

"Usually do. How'd you sleep?"

Apparently, Vivian never knew she had been tended throughout the night. Elizabeth chose not to bring it up. "I slept perfectly," she lied. "I'm looking forward to another beautiful day. Maybe it won't be so hot today." She'd be damned if she would admit to her discomfort and unhappiness at being here, the scare she had had in the night, and how worried she was about Vivian.

"After you're done packing, hitch up the team," Vivian told her. "The herd'll probably travel six or seven miles before the day's done. You'll have to bring the wagon up. Drive it east until you see a double rise in the land. It'll look like a woman lying on her back with big breasts resting to her sides. It's a real pretty place."

Elizabeth's cheeks flamed with the vivid

49

description. "I can find it." She tried to sound casual. "Good Lord," she whispered to herself after Vivian had departed. "That woman is downright primitive."

With the wagon packed to travel, Elizabeth went after the horses that had wandered over to the waterhole. She brought them back and tied them to a wagon wheel and then dragged the tack from beneath the wagon over to their sides.

The horses were skittish and would not stand still for the strange voice and the unfamiliar hands as Elizabeth struggled to slip on their bridles. They raised their big heads high out of her reach as she tried, one at a time, to force the bit between their long yellow teeth. Determined not to let them get the best of her, she placed a packing box in front of Skip. Resolutely, she grabbed his ear and yanked his head down, grunting with the effort, and rammed the bit between his teeth. She quickly slid the bridle over his ears and buckled it in place. She went after Mike the same way and then tossed a collar over his head. He nipped her on the bottom as she bent to adjust a strap. She yelled out in pain and slapped him smartly on the nose. As he jerked his head away, she snarled, "Damn you, Mike," this time making sure she faced him every moment.

It took her almost an hour to get the team ready, as she searched her memory to be sure buckles and straps were attached the same way today as yesterday. Fairly certain everything was in order, she backed the team between the wagon tongue, using the words *gee* and *haw* as she had heard her father use when backing his driving team into the carriage. Reluctantly, the horses responded to her no-nonsense handling of the reins and her authoritative commands, and she was glad that the words were commonly used.

She drove the wagon to the assigned spot, passing the herd at nine o'clock, waving to Vivian as she drove by. Arriving at twelve, she was thankful the trip was over. She had never driven a rig this size before, nor horses this rebellious as they repeatedly attempted to grab the bits between their teeth. Her fingers were cramped from having held the reins so tightly, and her jaw ached from grinding her teeth in nervousness.

Vivian had said nothing about nooning, but Elizabeth made a couple of sandwiches for her just in case. She waited until two and then sat and ate them alone. In another three hours she heard the first blatts of the sheep and the sharp barking of the dogs. The lonesome sounds drifted across the empty prairie, mixing with those of buzzing insects and an occasional bird calling out.

By six, Vivian joined her, signaling the dogs to keep the sheep nearby. "Howdy," she said.

"Howdy," Elizabeth answered, feeling just a little silly using such a quaint greeting.

"What's for supper?" Vivian grabbed the dipper and drank three cupfuls before she sat down in the wagon's shade. She removed her hat and wiped the sweat from her brow with the back of a sleeve. "Whew, it's a hot one."

"I made you some sandwiches, but I ate them."

"Sandwiches sound good. Can you make me a couple more? Make it three."

Elizabeth made five, and the women ate thick smoked beef sandwiches and drank lemonade. One by one, the dogs were tossed chunks of beef, each

51

carrying its share off to some secluded spot not far from the herd.

Vivian lay on the ground, propped up on an elbow. "Can you beat this life, Elizabeth? You're from a city, ain't you?"

"A big one. Crowds of people. Didn't Aunt Polly tell you?"

Vivian shook her head. "She didn't say much. Just that she had a niece coming to visit from the East." She stood and dusted off the seat of her pants. "How'd the team handle?"

"All right."

"Must be. You're here." Vivian looked at the sky. "Funny there ain't no wind. First time in a couple of months."

Elizabeth had noticed the lack of wind at about three this afternoon. She had not minded at all, in spite of the oppressive atmosphere.

Vivian walked back to the herd and worked it closer to the wagon, signaling the dogs to bunch them tighter. She returned and again drank from the dipper.

"Aren't the sheep awfully close to the wagon?" Elizabeth asked. Their smell was strong and pungent.

"Pretty close," Vivian replied. "Look over there." She pointed to the northwest. An ugly black cloud had formed and seemed to fill the greater part of the sky. Just then a blast of wind swooshed across the prairie. "We're in for it," she said. "You're going to have to help me, Elizabeth. Get your hat and grab those coats in the locker. Bring scarves, too. Wrap one around your head." She hurried toward the herd.

Elizabeth rushed into the wagon and grabbed the clothes. On the run, she jammed her arms through the sleeves of a bulky sheepskin coat and tied the scarf in place. She caught up to Vivian, passing her a scarf, speaking in a shaking voice. "I don't know what to do." Fear filled her chest as a strong gust of wind nearly knocked her off her feet. Swirling dust choked and blinded her. She fought to see, and wiped the dirt from her eyes.

Vivian anchored her hat and shouted above the noise of the wind as the milling sheep baaed nervously. "Just try to keep them muttonheads from scattering all over the prairie. As it is, we're gonna lose some. Hiya, dogs!" she yelled. "Samson, Tony!" She waved them to the far side of the herd. "Diamond, Jock, right!" The two dogs moved east, already tightening the circle, snapping at reluctant hooves and forcing the blatting animals in upon themselves.

All at once, foul weather came crashing down on the prairie. Hail half the size of eggs pelted Elizabeth. She cried out and tripped over a small unseen rock and fell to the ground, painfully striking her face against the earth. The taste of blood filled her mouth.

Vivian pulled her to her feet, yelling, "Move to the left, move to the left!" Elizabeth did, with hail brutally pounding her everywhere.

She raised her arms, shielding her head from the wrathful sky, and kept on moving. She ran along the outskirts of the herd, yelling and waving her arms, chasing after single sheep and small groups that had broken away from the larger one. Her dress tangled in her legs, and she held the skirt out of her way and then gave up, needing both hands. She tried to spot Vivian to see where she was and what she was

53

doing, but couldn't find her in a day turned nearly as dark as night.

The sky was now a rolling boil, and thunder and lightning filled the air. The hail, mixed with dollar-sized drops of rain, pelted everything in its path. Elizabeth didn't know how much longer she could endure the storm's continuous pounding. Her head ached and her arms felt as weighty as logs. She continuously waved first one and then the other in the heavy coat, trying to herd sheep and protect herself at the same time.

She could hardly hear herself yelling over the wind's howl and the crying sheep, which had become a mass of barely controlled hysteria. Their blatts and screams of terror filled her ears.

Now and then the high-pitched yap of a dog could be heard. They seemed to be everywhere at once, continuously circling the herd at break-neck speed. The dogs rapidly moved in and out of her sight as they snapped and barked at the heels of the sheep.

Elizabeth thought she must have run a hundred miles in her struggle to keep the flock from scattering. She saw one animal lying down, bleeding from the nose. She bent to lift it to its feet, but it was already dead. A little further on she saw another and then a third, all dead. Either the heavy downfall of hail or their own fright had killed them.

Elizabeth gasped for breath, her lungs on fire. She turned away from the wind, desperately needing to breathe freely for just a moment before facing the wild tempest again.

She ran along the outskirts of the herd for another five minutes and then, as suddenly as it had begun, the storm passed. She stopped to watch it recede rapidly toward the southeast, but Vivian was yelling at her to keep working, starting her moving again. With leaden legs, she ran after a bunch that had gotten past her, and was saved the job by Diamond, who was already turning them back.

The evening wore on as she and Vivian and the dogs rapidly circled the herd. Terror still gripped the sheep, but gradually the herders were able to slow their pace to a walk, speaking to the milling animals in low sounds. Vivian started to hum and then Elizabeth joined her. Softly, she sang "Onward Christian Soldiers," thankful she was still alive.

Vivian caught up with her once and kicked at a drift of hail piled against a dead sheep, scattering the ice. In a rage, she shouted, "Look at this mess. It's covered the land, and you can't drink one damn drop of it. Why the hell doesn't it rain, proper?"

Elizabeth felt Vivian's frustration as they moved along the herd, finding eight dead sheep. "There'll be a lot more by morning," Vivian said bitterly.

Chapter 4

The raging storm had cooled the air considerably.
The clouds had cleared off, exposing a thin sliver of
moon hanging high in the sky. Stars began to faintly
sprinkle the eastern horizon.

As they walked back to the wagon, Vivian glanced
at Elizabeth and frowned. "Your lip don't look too
good." She stopped and picked up a piece of hail.
"Here, hold this against it."

Tentatively, Elizabeth pressed the ice to her

mouth. She had been ignoring the dull ache in her front teeth and the pain in her upper lip.

At camp, the women found the canvas-topped wagon torn in several places and the horses missing. Angrily, Vivian said, "I told Al when he bought those devils they'd be no good in a storm. They're too damn spooky. At least they been grain fed. That'll bring them back by tomorrow. Come on with me."

Elizabeth followed Vivian into the wagon. "It's my fault the team is gone," she admitted ashamedly. "I should have hobbled them better."

"You will next time."

There isn't going to be a next time, Elizabeth vowed silently. Aching in every muscle, she laid aside her coat and hat and sank down on her cot.

Vivian lit a lantern and then rummaged through a small box, finally pulling out a needle and thread. "This ought to do it," she said. She poured some whiskey into a small bowl and dropped the needle and a length of thread into the fluid. "You have to be sewed up, Elizabeth."

"Sewed up?" Elizabeth exclaimed. "I thought you were going to repair the canvas." She had no idea that she was even badly hurt.

"It'll just take a couple of stitches." Vivian handed her a small mirror.

With dismay, Elizabeth studied the nasty-looking gash on her upper lip. The cut needed tending, all right, but by a doctor's trained hand, not that of a coarse sheepherder's. "I don't want you to sew me up," she stated flatly.

"It should be done. If it ain't, you're going to have an awful scar."

With trepidation, Elizabeth asked, "Have you ever sewed a person before?"

Vivian leaned toward the light and threaded the needle. "I've sewed a bunch of dresses."

"God . . . dresses." Elizabeth closed her eyes against the thought of being stitched together like a piece of cloth. "I need to lie down."

"In a minute, dear." Gently, Vivian washed the blood from Elizabeth's mouth and chin and then cleansed her lip with whiskey. "I'd rather have pure alcohol," she said, "but this'll do just as well."

Elizabeth gritted her teeth against the pain and clutched the buffalo robe beneath her until her fingers ached. "It stings, Vivian."

"Quit complaining or I'll sew both your lips together permanent. You can take it. You got a Yankee heart. You said so. That's as tough as a Montana heart, ain't it? Now take a good, stiff swallow of this stuff."

Vivian handed Elizabeth a half cup of whiskey. She brought the cup to her lips and swallowed fast. The fire from the hard spirits searing her throat and stomach matched that of the fire in her lip. She would have screamed aloud, but a sudden fit of coughing attacked her and she fought for air, her eyes wide open and raining tears. She tried to breathe around fumes of alcohol still lingering in her mouth and filtering up her nose and down her throat. Vivian slapped her on the back and held and rocked her until she could breathe normally again. Dazed, Elizabeth leaned heavily against Vivian, wondering if the horror of this nightmare was going to go on forever.

Vivian eased Elizabeth back, saying, "Lay down

58

now, and I'll fix you up in no time." She pinched the wound closed and passed the needle through Elizabeth's skin.

Again there was pain, and Elizabeth's stomach heaved as she felt the thread being dragged through her flesh. She was panicky and claustrophobic as Vivian hunched over her, talking in a low voice about nonsensical things. Elizabeth clung to Vivian's prattle in a desperate effort to forget the nausea and burning sensation lingering in her stomach and the newer and more piercing one left behind by the needle and thread.

"One more," Vivian said. She was quick and efficient, and soon she was done. She inspected the stitches carefully and then handed Elizabeth a cup of whiskey. "Here, take another drink. It'll help you relax."

Nothing short of death would help Elizabeth relax, but she obediently took the cup. The alcohol touched the wound, burning a second time like live embers as it slid past her lips and down her throat. She could not stop the fresh tears that sprang to her eyes as she handed Vivian the empty cup and fell back onto the cot.

"You're gonna be just fine, dear," Vivian whispered softly. She wiped away Elizabeth's tears with her bandanna. "You ought to leave the stitches in for a week." She studied her handiwork one more time and then said, "If it'll make you feel any better, Henry will probably return early in the morning to check on the stock. Most likely, he'll bring your buggy, thinking you've had enough. He's pretty thoughtful that way."

Vivian stayed with Elizabeth while the worst of

the pain passed. The whiskey was working now, and Elizabeth felt as if she were floating just above the robe. Nothing seemed to be touching her except Vivian's warm hand. It was comforting to lie there while the sheepherder repeatedly smoothed back her hair and ran a rough palm down her cheek.

"I need to check the herd," Vivian finally said. "I'll be back soon. You rest."

Elizabeth dozed for a while, and when she awoke, she found Vivian sitting before a campfire. Elizabeth joined her and stood gazing into the flames.

"How you feeling?" Vivian asked.

Elizabeth drew up a box and sat down. "I've had better days." Her lip felt as big as a wagon wheel, and it hurt to talk.

"Most of the sheep have bedded down," Vivian said. "Some are still restless. I'll have to go out a couple more times, and then I'll be in to stay the night."

Elizabeth nodded. "Anything you want me to do?"

"Just go to bed."

"Of course." Elizabeth was more than willing. And she could not wait for Henry to come tomorrow.

The following morning, Henry arrived driving Elizabeth's buggy, just as Vivian had predicted. With as little talk as possible, Elizabeth cooked a final breakfast for three and then collected her bag from the wagon. After a brief farewell, she drove directly toward the soddy. She had a twenty-mile journey ahead of her, and she could not wait to reach its end.

Just as she had thanked Vivian last night for

caring for her, Elizabeth had expected Vivian would, in turn, thank her this morning for all her help. But she waited in vain. Vivian never mentioned her aid, leaving Elizabeth to wonder how Vivian could be so insensitive.

Elizabeth's desire to be independent was still strong in her. But the greater need to pull herself together before going back to the Box R was what took her to the soddy now.

She arrived by late morning, first putting Billy in the corral and then going to the backhouse. Still several yards from the building, she began to yell. She approached cautiously and at the door banged loudly to drive any lurking snakes deep into the rock foundation. Before leaving, she stamped on the floor several times and shouted once more. She would feel ridiculous if anyone observed her actions, but she was not going to be surprised by a snake again.

Within the cool soddy, she was struck by overwhelming weariness. Constantly aware of the throbbing in her lip, she wanted only to sleep and forget the pain for a while. She lay down, intending to remove her boots in a couple of minutes, and fell asleep thinking that she ought to get up and do it.

She awoke at nine that night. By lantern light, she put Billy in the barn, feeling terribly guilty that he had had to endure the heat of the day without water or shelter. She quickly completed her chores and then returned to sleep away the rest of the night and half the next day. She rose gritty-eyed, blinking the cobwebs from her brain. She felt dirty and rumpled and ravenous. She ate and took care of Billy and then slept again. That night she ate once more and by eight o'clock was back in bed. She was going to be overdue at the ranch, but she would stay at least three more days. She would also need to ration her remaining food and supplies.

She was fairly relaxed at the soddy this time. Perhaps because she had spent most of her time sleeping during the day, she therefore found it unnecessary to face empty hours with nothing to do. But she didn't think so. She wondered if she was adjusting to Montana's solitude. She even considered the possibility of spending a cold winter's night here, just to see what it would be like.

She stayed a full week before going home. Her lip was healing nicely and the swelling was gone. Vivian Blake — sheepherder — had done an excellent job.

Upon arising this final morning, Elizabeth tried not to think about the task before her: removing the stitches. She washed her face and hands and swallowed hard as she sat at the table. She propped a hand mirror against a lantern to catch the morning light and peered into it, studying the stitches and considering the best way to snip them. Her hand shook as she raised tiny scissors to her lip. Ignoring the queasiness in her stomach, she cut first one stitch and then the other. Now all that was left was to pull them out. With tweezers, she tugged slightly at a stitch. The skin had grown around the thread, anchoring it within her flesh.

"Oh, God," she cried. "I can't *do* this! Aunt Polly will have to do it!" She slammed the tweezers down on the table, knocking over the mirror. Tears welled up in her eyes; angrily she brushed them away. She absolutely could *not* go to the ranch with clipped stitches sticking out of her upper lip! The unpleasant job of removing them was hers alone to face.

Resolutely, she again took up the tweezers. Once more, she pulled tentatively at a thread. The stitch was not going to come out easily. She was going to have to give it a good, firm yank. She drew back her lip, tightening it against her teeth and snatched out the thread. The pain was sharp and then it was over. She did not stop to think, but went after the second stitch the same way. Tiny drops of blood oozed from the punctures, but the rest of her skin looked fine. She smiled and blotted her lip dry.

Now she could go to the Box R.

In heavy sweaters, Elizabeth and Polly sat in rockers on the front porch. Elizabeth had arrived just before dark. The stars shone clear and bright in a sky as black as pitch. The only earthly illumination was a weak rectangle of lantern light cast upon the ground through an open window from behind them.

"Look, there goes another one!" Elizabeth pointed to a shooting star sailing across the heavens. "I could sit here all night and just watch this lovely show."

"I do, now and then," Polly answered. Her rocker squeaked rhythmically, creating a hypnotic lullaby. She sighed audibly and stilled her chair. "What will you write your parents, Elizabeth? They'll be upset about your mouth. I don't know how you're going to explain this."

"Why should I say anything? I got caught out in a storm. It isn't anyone's fault. My face will look fine by the time I return home."

"Vivian Blake had no business taking you along."

"I thought I was going as company."

"Good heavens, Elizabeth! A single herder can only shepherd about three thousand sheep at a time. Vivian has plenty more than that. I'm surprised and disappointed that she thought you could take the place of her hired man — and you let her get away with it." The rocker began to creak angrily. "A couple of other women hereabouts own their own ranches and think exactly like she does. I've met them in town a time or two. The lot of them think alike, but Vivian's the worst."

"I did all right, Aunt Polly. I did very well, as a matter of fact." How could her aunt think this way? Polly herself was an incredibly hard-working woman.

"Vivian was wrong, Elizabeth," Polly retorted sharply. The rocker increased its speed. "We have a general rule here. When you go visiting, you're expected to help out while you're there — unless you're childbearing."

"Aunt Polly!"

"Keep it in mind, Elizabeth. There isn't free time out here like there is back in your father's fine house. So beware if someone invites you to visit. You can end up doing some mighty backbreaking work."

"I work at home, Aunt Polly."

"Polishing silver and setting table isn't work. What you did out on that range is work! Don't get mixed up in it. Jonathan won't want his wife scarred up like a bowery gal with callouses on her hands."

"He won't know anything about it until he sees me. And don't write my parents I spend time in a soddy, either."

"I'll keep still, but you'd better watch what you do hereafter. Do you want to explain why you were late?"

"I wanted to look the same to you and Uncle Andy as when I left a week ago."

"A week and a half ago," Polly corrected. "And you don't look the same."

Obviously. But Elizabeth thought she had come close. She refused to get drawn into another discussion about it. She had apologized repeatedly for her tardiness when she had arrived. It should have been enough.

Polly's rocker slowed to sing to the night again. "I'm going to be hoeing this place out for the next few days. I want my home to be clean when winter sets in, and I'd like you to help me. It won't be backbreaking work, either."

"You'll have to tell me what to do," Elizabeth said, wishing her family's servants were here.

"Don't worry, young lady," Polly replied, reaching out and patting her on the knee. "I will."

Polly's gesture reminded Elizabeth of the time when Vivian had patted her knee as they rode the wagon, and she felt a tiny quaking in her heart. Could she possibly still consider Vivian some sort of friend? The woman had used her so.

And yet, she had been strangely kind and gentle, and had called her "dear."

"Then let's go to bed," Polly said, bringing Elizabeth back to the present. "We'll start first thing in the morning."

She rose and stretched, and Elizabeth followed her into the house.

Chapter 5

In the barn at Vivian's old homestead, Billy munched grain in a box stall. Elizabeth hummed a little tune and curried his broad back with long strokes, the teeth of the tool leaving neat rows of tiny furrows in his hair. He swung his strong head around to nuzzle her.

A shadow in the door stretched across the dusty floor, the backlight creating a small silhouette outlining a wide-brimmed hat, boots, pants, and a thick coat covering Vivian's small body. A flash of pleasure filled Elizabeth as she paused mid-stroke. "Vivian! What are you doing here?"

"Hadn't seen you in so long, I came to visit," Vivian answered. "Unless you're busy."

Elizabeth suddenly lost interest in Billy, coming over to greet Vivian with an impulsive kiss on the cheek. Vivian reddened, making Elizabeth wonder if perhaps she shouldn't have done such a thing. Vivian put a hand on Elizabeth's arm, and on tiptoes, kissed Elizabeth's cheek as well.

Shyly, they looked at each other, Elizabeth at a loss for words.

Vivian cleared her throat. "I stopped at the Box R. Polly told me you were here."

"About half the time," Elizabeth answered. "As long as I go home very other day or so, Polly and Andy don't worry about me being alone. Andy drops by on the days I'm not there."

Vivian cocked her head to one side. "Why do you keep coming back? What do you do with your time?"

"Oh, the same old thing," Elizabeth replied. "I read and reread. I knit, too. I never knew how before, but Aunt Polly taught me a few stitches. I think the biggest thing I do is listen to the quietness. I never heard such silence before I came to Montana. It bothered me a great deal the first time I stayed here. I've grown to like it and shall miss it when I return to New York." She bolted the stall door and picked up her hat. "Can you stay? I've fresh coffee."

"I could use some," Vivian replied enthusiastically.

Their breath led the way in a misty cloud as they walked to the soddy. In front was Vivian's wagon, loaded with boxes and bags.

"Winter supplies," she explained. "I've been to Billings."

Incredulously, Elizabeth asked, "You drove to Billings all alone?" It was a two-day journey!

Vivian nodded, apparently taking her trip as a matter of course. She said, "Al and Henry are with the sheep till the end of November. Then the three of us will move the herd to winter camp near the base of Bull Mountain. Better shelter through the snowing." Just outside the door, Vivian stopped to study a huge pile of coal. "You ain't planning to stay here through the winter, are you?"

"That's Uncle Andy's idea of helping me get through that terribly cold night a couple of weeks ago. I'll bet it was a hundred degrees the day it was delivered. Anyway, if more than five snowflakes gather in one place," Elizabeth assured her, "Billy and I will be on the road."

"You better make sure of that, Elizabeth. We have wicked winters here."

And yet, Vivian had gone to Billings *alone*. What about the danger in that, Elizabeth silently challenged.

Inside, the house was warm and snug. The women tossed their wraps onto the bed. Looking pale and tired, Vivian took a seat before the stove, opening its door and leaning into the heat.

Concerned, Elizabeth asked, "Are you all right? Can I get you something to eat?" She handed Vivian a mug of coffee.

Vivian took a sip and nodded. She slowly rolled the hot cup between her hands as if to collect its heat and store it within her palms. "It's this side of mine," she said. "It kicked up a couple of days ago. It's a lot better now. It was hell for a while riding that wagon seat."

Elizabeth put a frypan on the stove and threw in some lard. The grease snapped and splattered as she added two eggs. "I can't imagine doing the work you do," she said. "How did you get started?"

Vivian propped her worn boots against the stove door. "Tom bought five hundred head of sheep from a herder when we first came here. But Al and Henry are *partidos*. They get a percentage of the herd's increase after lambing season. Al will probably leave with his share, he's built up enough stock. But I expect Henry will stay on."

Elizabeth slid the eggs onto a plate and added two thick slabs of bread. She handed the plate to Vivian. "It sounds like an impossible job to me."

Vivian nodded her thanks. "Not once you're used to it." She began to tackle the eggs, mumbling, "Your lip looks just fine. Who took out the stitches?"

"I did."

Vivian smiled. "Good. I was hoping you would. How did Polly and Andy take it?"

"Not well at all. Polly said I was not to get hurt nor work like a fool. Sensible words. Andy swore his head off, threatening to shoot every sheepherder within a hundred-mile radius."

"He gets cantankerous."

"He says sheep destroy the range and poison the water holes."

"That's fools' talk. Them sheep won't spoil the range with good management. As for poisoning waterholes, cattlemen think the glands between sheeps' toes give off a bad smell and leave the smell

70

at waterholes, so the cattle won't drink. It ain't true, but you can't tell a cattleman that." Vivian helped herself to another cup of coffee. "You never came back to Sheephaven."

"I am no help as a guest."

"Why, you surely are, Elizabeth. I'd like you to come again. I won't work you this time. You can tell your Aunt Polly I said so. She knows me well enough to know I never say a word I don't mean."

Elizabeth chuckled. "You should hear the girls and me chatter back home. Half of what we say isn't worth listening to."

"Probably less than that, I'm thinkin'."

Defending her friends, Elizabeth answered irritably. "But that's for me to say, isn't it?"

"I suppose," Vivian replied, then quickly added, "But you're all right. Made out of tough leather. I've seen other ladies come visiting from the East. I've even had a few to the ranch. They were nothing like you."

"And how am I?"

"I don't know. Not so much fluff as appears. I can't tolerate too much fluff. For myself, that is."

"I love fluff." Elizabeth pulled a chair over to the stove. Daintily, she adjusted her skirt before sitting down. "I love frilly dresses, ten starched petticoats worn at once . . . although I can't dress that way here."

"That kind of dress would blow clean over your head."

"That's already happened. The first day I arrived. Uncle Andy nearly died with laughter, I nearly died of embarrassment."

Vivian set aside her empty plate and brushed the

crumbs from her lap. "I still don't take with too much fluff. Slows me down."

Elizabeth sighed deeply. "I shall be glad to dress that way again. And after being here . . . living here . . ." She glanced around the soddy. "Life will seem like child's play once I return home."

"I'd like to stay home more, myself. When Tom was alive I used to bake pies. I'm a fair pie maker. Especially apple. Used to win prizes in Kentucky with my apple pies."

"I can fry eggs and bacon and grits and potatoes, and that's about all. We have a regular cook and I never —"

"A regular cook? Your mother don't cook?"

"Not much. Now and then when Cook Broody is sick, she'll put something together for Father and me."

"Waste of time," Vivian said pointedly. "You ought to know how to cook more than what you do."

"I've always eaten."

"Woman's ways. Somebody's always looking out for you."

"I am a woman, Vivian."

A constrained silence fell between them.

After a length of time, Vivian spoke. "You're rich, ain't you?"

Elizabeth answered with an embarrassed silence.

"I don't understand why you're livin' in this old sod heap then," the sheepherder said. "Is it just so's you can go back home and tell everybody how you roughed it when you were in Montana?"

Elizabeth shifted uncomfortably. "I'd like to know

that I'm able to do some difficult things, to feel I have worth."

Vivian stared at Elizabeth. "Didn't know you had any doubts. Besides, I already know how much worth you got. Knew it the day I saw you bustin' sod."

Her compliment pleased Elizabeth, allowing her to forgive Vivian her personal judgments against her.

Vivian stood and shook down her pants legs. "I gotta be heading home. Just wanted to be sure you were still alive."

The women donned their coats and walked outside. Vivian climbed onto the wagon and slipped on leather work gloves.

How gracefully she handles herself, Elizabeth thought, no matter what she does.

Vivian drew her hat low over her eyes and took up the reins. She released the brake and said, "Why don't you come out early tomorrow, and we'll go up to winter camp together. It's not too far. I have to go, anyway."

"I'd love to."

Vivian tipped a hand to the brim of her hat, looking very cavalier, then pointed the wagon north.

For an instant, Elizabeth envied her, her easy manners and simple living. She watched Vivian bump along the road until she was a speck in the distance.

Soon after Vivian was out of sight, Elizabeth packed and went home to let Polly know she would be staying with Vivian for a couple of days and to assure her that this time she would not be working.

"Don't let her trick you into anything, Elizabeth," Polly warned sternly.

"Don't worry, Aunt Polly," Elizabeth promised. "I'm through being a sheepherder."

By eleven o'clock the following morning Elizabeth arrived at Sheephaven. She drew the buggy up beside Vivian's horse, the animal saddled and ready at the rail. Saddlebags were stuffed and a bedroll was tied behind the cantle. A questioning frown furrowed her brow as she jumped from the buggy.

Vivian came out of the soddy. " 'Bout time . . . why, you ain't got on pants." Crossly, she asked, "You got a divided skirt with you?"

Flustered, Elizabeth said, "I . . . I have none. I assumed we'd take the buggy. You said it wasn't far."

"It ain't short, neither. Go on inside and get some pants and boots out of the closet. Tom's clothes hang there, still. There'll be something in there that'll do. There's some beans and bacon and coffee on the stove. You'll be hungry before long. We're late, so I'll saddle Billy for you." She led the horse and buggy away.

Sharply reproved, Elizabeth watched Vivian walk stiffly away. Since when was eleven o'clock not early? Goodness, things never got moving at her house for social visits before two PM. She thought she had been *very* early. And how was she supposed to have known they would be riding horses? Good Lord, she had never even sat on the back of a horse, let alone ridden one! How she wished now that she had listened to her father the dozens of times he had encouraged her to learn.

She hurried inside and scrambled to change into the unfamiliar clothing. She had never worn pants before, and they felt uncomfortable as she drew them on. But she wasted no time and was sitting at the table, gobbling her food, afraid not to be ready by the time Vivian returned. Had she any spunk, Elizabeth thought, she would put her dress right back on and drive away from here.

"Ready?"

Hunched over her plate as she rushed to finish eating, she hadn't seen Vivian come in. The herder's voice made her jump. Elizabeth snarled, angry that Vivian could do that to her. "No, I'm not ready. I haven't finished my coffee."

"Sure. Take your time." Vivian opened her pocketwatch and deliberately stared at it. She sat at the table casually drumming her fingers.

Elizabeth had a second cup, and when she had finished, stood, saying, "Now I'm ready."

"Have to do the dishes first." Vivian looked a second time at her watch.

"Let's hurry, then," Elizabeth said, trying to grab hold of the situation, and not let Vivian rule her every moment.

At last it was time to leave, and a rush of nervous excitement coursed through Elizabeth's veins.

Just before mounting Vivian said, "We'll be gone about four days."

"Four days?" Instantly, Elizabeth thought of Polly. Her aunt would kill her! But it was too late to do anything about it now — unless she went home. No, Elizabeth decided, she didn't want to do that. Let it be four days, and hang Aunt Polly.

And she'd be dashed before she would let Vivian's

75

little surprises upset her anymore. Let the woman do or say whatever she wished. Elizabeth put aside her growing discontent and, holding both reins, tightly grabbed the saddle horn.

"Other side," Vivian said.

"Other side?"

"You mount from the left."

Elizabeth hadn't ever paid much attention to how riders got on their horses, but now that she thought about it . . . Flustered, she walked to the left side of Billy.

She put a foot into a stirrup, and with a little bounce, swung her free leg. Her boot caught beneath the bedroll tied to the cantle. Elizabeth hung for a moment, nearly tumbling backwards, before freeing her leg and continuing her swing. She glanced to see if her clumsiness had been observed, but Vivian was pointedly looking at something on the ground to her right.

Astride the saddle, Elizabeth felt awkward, her legs unaccustomedly spread. It was unnerving and embarrassing. Ladies did *not* spread their legs. "Do you have a sidesaddle?" she asked.

"In the barn. Must have two inches of dust on it. Want it?"

Vivian made her feel foolish. "No. Let's go."

As they rode, Vivian offered advice on how to sit on the saddle, the direction to point toes, and how to handle reins. Elizabeth adjusted her body accordingly, trying to do well. She didn't feel very comfortable, but, she thought, an hour of riding should make her feel better.

In another hour, Elizabeth did not feel better. She didn't feel good at all. She needed to stop and stretch. For too long she had been holding her knees at an unfamiliar angle. The insides of her legs hurt, and her hip joints felt as though someone were slowly and methodically twisting them out of their sockets. Worse, she needed to seek the shelter of a tree, or a rock, or *something*. But this place was bare of nature's usual ornaments. Somehow Montana had been left out of the grand design Elizabeth was so used to seeing in the East: trees and shrubs — thick shrubs. How was she to ask Vivian to stop? Should she just say: "Vivian, I need to use the necessary room?" The Montanan would laugh her right out of the saddle. Gripping the horn, Elizabeth gallantly ignored her discomfort.

"How about working these broomtails a bit?" Vivian suggested, and touched her mount in the flanks. The horse picked up speed, Vivian smoothly raising and lowering with the saddle, looking like part of both the leather and the horse.

Elizabeth nudged Billy into motion as Vivian had done. She tried to sit as Vivian was sitting, struggled to stay close to the saddle, but she was sure there were yards of daylight between herself and the seat. Smack, smack, smack. Her bottom hit with painful jolts as she careened from side to side while gripping Billy with legs too tired to be of much use. She desperately clutched the horn and reins with both hands, no longer caring in which direction Billy was heading, as long as she didn't fall out of the saddle.

Billy caught up with the mare, and Vivian reached out and grabbed his bridle, bringing both horses to a stop. Nimbly, she jumped from the saddle. "Let's get down and walk for a while."

Elizabeth thought those the most sensible words

77

she had ever heard spoken. Using the pommel for support, she slid slowly to the ground.

Vivian came to her side and helped her down. "Are you all right?" she asked.

"Right as rain," came the clipped reply. While Vivian watched, Elizabeth took several shaky steps. Her legs didn't feel right. They felt like they were still wrapped around the horse. They felt as if they were bowed! She looked down, surprised to see that they were as straight as they had been when she began her ride a little more than an hour ago. "I'm fine," she insisted.

Vivian moved back to her mount, and for a while the women walked. Eventually, Vivian suggested they ride again.

Elizabeth knew she could not possibly get back on Billy. The terrible pressure of her bladder made all other discomforts in her life totally unimportant. "I must use the necessary room," she blurted. She waited for Vivian's laughter.

Deadpan, Vivian said, "Other side of the horses."

Partially concealed by the animals, Elizabeth could barely make her legs work properly as she lowered and then raised herself. She wished this journey were over, unable to envision another three days of riding facing her. She returned to Billy's side.

"I never drink coffee if I have to ride far," Vivian said. "Too uncomfortable."

Coldly, Elizabeth answered, "It's good of you to tell me."

"But we can stop any time you need to."

"That's fine."

"In an emergency, you wouldn't stop."

"Of course not."

"But now . . . anytime."

Elizabeth could no longer conceal her rising irritation. "Why, in heaven's name, don't you tell me more things, Vivian; *little* things that would help me get along better out here. My life would be so much easier."

"What kinds of things?" Vivian was already in the saddle, waiting.

Hand on the pommel, correctly standing on the left side of Billy, Elizabeth looked at Vivian from across her saddle. "Like not drinking coffee before a long ride. Like showing me how to start a fire in the stove before leaving me alone in the soddy to nearly kill Henry with smoke. And you might have warned me that there would be mice there, not to mention the rest of Montana's unexpected quirks."

"How much more do you think you gained by finding all this out by yourself?"

"But I would have been better prepared to face these obstacles."

"That's not true, I'm thinkin'." Vivian tugged at her hat brim and leaned against the saddle horn. "You throw a person into a situation, he learns about himself. Let him sit around and think about what *might* happen, he worries himself right out of trying something new. If I'd told you mice might run across your face in the night, would you've stayed at the soddy? If you'd known how bad a hail storm could be, would you've been brave enough to come with me? And did you know you could cook with cats and chips? Maybe you can't roast a pig or a lamb, but you're good enough to make simple food taste better than leather. Hell, that's just little stuff anyway. Nothing worth mentioning — unless you're a real inexperienced person. Greenhorns we call 'em."

"I know what they're called, Vivian. Do you always believe yourself so infernally correct?"

"Nope," she said, urging her horse forward. "But don't make me wrong about you."

Elizabeth hurried to catch the loping rider ahead of her and thought of Aunt Polly and how she had promised her aunt that she wouldn't let Vivian trick her into doing any work. Well, she sure felt like she was working right now.

At sundown, they stopped near a small stream. Vivian collected fuel, and Elizabeth cooked beans and biscuits, aching in every muscle. After cleanup, Vivian staked the horses and showed Elizabeth how to lay out her bedroll and use her saddle for a pillow. Tired as Elizabeth was, the stones poking through the blanket and the hardness of her pillow did not bother her. She drew the blanket tightly to her throat, burying her chin in the warmth of the thick sheepskin coat Vivian had rolled in her blanket this morning. Laying her hat over her face, she shut out the glistening stars above. In minutes she was asleep, never hearing the lonesome songs of the coyotes drifting mournfully across the empty plains.

The following morning, Elizabeth awoke stiff as a board. She had never dreamed that horseback riding could be so painful an experience. The ladies and gentlemen she had seen as she strolled through Central Park rode their big animals side by side, cantering gracefully by. They had laughed and chatted, looking as comfortable as if they were sitting in rocking chairs. Right now, Elizabeth hated them all.

There was little talk between the women as Elizabeth prepared breakfast, gritting her teeth as she moved about. Vivian carefully handed her four eggs she had packed in biscuit flour, and Elizabeth fried the eggs and baked a flat unleavened bread to dip into the yolks.

Vivian sopped up the yellow mass with a piece of bread and stuffed it into her mouth. "You're a better cook than Henry or Al. But don't tell them I told you."

The hard-won compliment pleased Elizabeth. Three months ago, she couldn't have cooked outdoors. Three months ago she wouldn't have touched a cow chip.

She looked up from her plate to catch Vivian intently gazing at her. Vivian reached out a hand, softly laying it against her cheek. She said, "I'm awful proud of the way you handled yourself yesterday. You're a game lady."

Something slammed into Elizabeth's heart.

A half hour later, they were on their way. Elizabeth looked into Vivian's smiling eyes, and the pain in her sore body seemed to melt away.

They reached the mountain camp by late afternoon, having stopped off and on throughout the day to stretch their legs and to munch jerky and drink from canteens. With Vivian's help, Elizabeth slipped wearily from the saddle.

81

The sod house they entered was much like her own. She was surprised to see that it was well stocked with canned goods, lanterns, fuel, blankets, cookware, a cook stove, and, although crude, a big bed and a table with stools. "You could move right in," she remarked.

Vivian lifted the lid of the woodbox just outside the door. "I don't think anyone has used the place this summer. Usually someone comes by, a cowboy, a gold digger, a rustler. I won't have to do anything to get the place ready except check the walls and bring in winter supplies." Vivian turned at the door. "We might as well eat now. I'll bring in the saddlebags."

Elizabeth sank to the bed and lay down. She thought she would rest only a minute or two, to wait for that awful bowlegged sensation to disappear before tackling her duties. The next thing she knew, the soddy was filled with the golden light of several lanterns and deliciously appetizing smells from a pot bubbling on the stove. She groaned as she sat up.

"How you feeling?" Vivian sat near the stove.

"I do keep giving you occasion to ask that question, don't I?" Elizabeth bent over her legs, trying to ease her tight back muscles. "I'm sorry I fell asleep. I know I should have had food on the table by now."

"Why?" Vivian asked. "There are two women here."

"Since you took care of the horses, it's only fair that I cook."

"You don't have to cook if you don't want to. I thought you wanted to."

Elizabeth stood and stretched before moving to the stove. "Whatever gave you that idea?"

"You jumped right in last night, and when we camped before, too."

"I thought I was supposed to. That's the idea I was given."

"Henry or me could have cooked. We would've been glad to."

Elizabeth felt a rising anger. "You mean to tell me, Vivian Blake, that I had a choice out there?"

"Naturally. We all take turns. Every day somebody different cooks."

"Well, I don't remember being given a choice!"

"You didn't ask."

"Damn it, Vivian, I wasn't told I *had* a choice."

"Didn't think you needed to be told something like that. I ain't your mother to tell you everything you can or can't do."

Elizabeth flushed.

"You're in Montana now, Elizabeth. Make your own decisions."

Elizabeth drew up a stool and sat down. "I have made several decisions since coming here."

"Make more." Vivian lifted the lid of the pot. She stirred its contents and then set the table while Elizabeth closed her eyes and dreamed of her New York home.

She thought of the fire in the great fireplace in the reading room. If she were there, she would be comfortably sitting before it now, sipping hot cocoa that had been served to her. Her mother would be crocheting while her father pored over the evening paper. It would be quiet except for the clip-clopping of passing cabbies and surreys. The doorbell would ring and Jonathan would stop by. He would sit beside her and also drink cocoa. They would talk about his day at his factory, and she would enjoy listening. It would be nice hearing his deep voice resonant in the room.

Jonathan would rave like a madman when he learned how she had lived in Montana. Yet, it would be so much fun to have something to discuss with him other than the latest ladies' tea she had attended. She would enjoy describing to him this feisty woman who sat idly stirring stew and who both enchanted and infuriated her.

"What are you thinking about?" Vivian asked.

"Home."

"Thought so. Put on your coat. We'll go for a walk while the pot simmers."

Elizabeth paused. "No, Vivian, I don't think I will go for a walk. I don't want to, and I'm not going to."

The sheepherder pursed her lips and studied the hard-packed floor. "Elizabeth," she said quietly. "Would you care to go for a short walk with me?"

Elizabeth smiled coyly. "How nice of you to ask."

It took a few minutes for Elizabeth's legs to loosen up as they strolled beneath the blazing stars. Behind them the mountains created a black backdrop, solid but for the outline of their low, worn peaks. The rising moon splashed a silver ocean across the prairie floor, and the sharp air made the women rub their arms with their hands.

"I only come out here alone a couple of times a year," Vivian said. "I love its solitude."

"It is . . ." Elizabeth could not find words to explain the peaceful quietness within her. She linked her arm through Vivian's as they walked.

At some point they turned to each other. Vivian

was so strong and steady. Elizabeth was sure she would be someone to lean on in time of great need, someone who would never let her down.

Vivian drew close to Elizabeth, holding her tightly, resting her head against Elizabeth's shoulder. Elizabeth's arms slid around Vivian.

They did not speak and did not move for a long time. Elizabeth could smell the horse Vivian had ridden all day, and the odor of sheep from the coat she wore. The sheep smells were not disagreeable any more. Perhaps it was because the odor was part of Vivian. Elizabeth chuckled, breaking their spell.

Vivian stepped back. "What's so funny?"

"I don't think funny is the right word. Happy would suit me better." Elizabeth linked her arm through Vivian's again, and they continued on. "I laugh because I am happy."

"I'm happy, too," Vivian replied. "I haven't felt this happy in a long, long time. It's a nice feeling. I'd forgotten."

They returned to the cabin and ate quietly. Afterward, Vivian tossed Elizabeth a nightgown. "I didn't know if you knew you'd be gone overnight, so I brought this along just in case."

"You could have mentioned it. I would still have come."

"After your last trip with me, I didn't want to take the chance you might not."

Elizabeth slipped into the gown, shyly turning her back to Vivian. She glanced toward Vivian who unselfconsciously cast her pants and shirt aside. She wore only a pair of drawers trimmed with lace cuffs reaching to mid-calf and no binding cloth to hold her small breasts. As Vivian reached for her gown, muscles rippled across her back and down her small shoulders and arms.

Elizabeth could not resist commenting, "You're very strong. All that hard work . . ."

Vivian sat before the stove and fed the fire one more time. She closed the door and propped her elbows on her knees, her gown creating a tent between her legs. "I do the same as everybody does out here, Elizabeth. Work like hell dawn to dusk, then fall into bed dead tired at night and then get up the next morning and do it all over again." She paused, looking thoughtful. "I suppose it's a slow way to die, a hard way. But I owe no man, no one tells me what to do or how to do it. I ain't got a lot of money, but I'm thinkin' I'm at least as rich as you. Don't take that as a criticism, Elizabeth. It's just another way to look at living."

Elizabeth climbed into bed, the mattress tick rustling beneath her. The smell of hay assailed her nostrils. "My first experience with Montana feathers," she said.

Vivian closed the damper on the stove and turned out the lanterns, making her way to the bed by the glow of dying wicks. She climbed beneath the blanket. "I stuffed the tick with fresh grass before I left in the spring. It held up pretty good, didn't it?"

Their shoulders touched as they settled beneath the covers. Neither moved away, and Elizabeth found herself thinking how cozy it would be to snuggle next to Vivian. She felt Vivian's hand rest lightly on her shoulder, and awkwardly she covered it with her own. Vivian burrowed her head beneath Elizabeth's chin and into the hollow of her shoulder.

Elizabeth stroked Vivian's hair, listening to her

murmurs of contentment. She slid a hand down Vivian's back and around her waist and then lay very, very still to quell the rapid triggering of her heart as Vivian slowly rubbed her back.

Hours later, she estimated, she finally fell asleep.

Chapter 6

Elizabeth woke stiff and sore. But her discomforts were endurable and nearly forgotten in the strong arms of Vivian Blake.

Elizabeth had liked sleeping next to Vivian, had liked it a lot. She had slept with a cousin or two as a child, and remembered with nostalgia spending half the night tee-heeing and talking before she finally settled down. But she was no longer a child, and her feelings were entirely different; they were more intense, more . . . meaningful. Elizabeth recalled how madly her heart had raced as Vivian rubbed her back and breathed heavily into her hair. She wondered if there would ever come a time in the future when the two of them might once again sleep together, deeply nestled beneath warm blankets, lying quietly in the night, feeling close to one another.

Elizabeth propped herself up on one elbow and studied the sleeping woman. Vivian's breathing was deep and steady. Looking peaceful and childlike, Vivian slept with her right hand curled in a ball against her cheek, the thumb tucked securely within the palm. A surge of love for Vivian struck Elizabeth with an unrecognizable force, and she leaned toward her and kissed her on the cheek.

Vivian stirred and then awoke. She smiled and yawned widely. "Lordy, you can see your breath with no trouble this morning. I'm going to hate to crawl out of this nice warm bed." She fanned away the mist before her. "I woke up off and on in the night," she said. She looked at Elizabeth, who had retreated beneath the blankets, and her voice took on a serious tone. "All I could think of was you sleeping in that soddy all by yourself. It's time you got out of there, Elizabeth. Winter's coming on fast."

"My, my, you even wake up thinking practical thoughts."

"I worry about you."

"Uncle Andy and Aunt Polly have asked me to come home permanently this week."

"You better listen to them, Elizabeth. They ain't no fools. Don't treat them as such."

"I only wanted to stay as long as possible."

"It ain't possible any longer. When we get back, you go straight home."

"I promise."

89

Vivian lay back and laced her fingers together, propping her hands behind her head. "I wish we had a maid to stoke up the fire and bring us a cup of coffee."

"I don't want anyone here but us."

"Neither do I," Vivian agreed.

They lay staring at the ceiling, watching their breath float and dissipate in the cold room.

"Do you know, Elizabeth," Vivian said thoughtfully, "that you know more about me than I do about you, and that ain't fair . . . except I do know how darned stubborn you can be." She dipped under the covers again and against Elizabeth's side. Elizabeth felt her shiver.

"If you think about it," Elizabeth said, "we really haven't had much chance to talk. What would you like to know?"

"How rich girls live, I expect. I don't know what else to ask. I don't even know how they dress, except from pictures in the catalogs. And mine's a year old."

"I have a mother and a father," Elizabeth began. "And we live in a very large house. I have no brothers, but there was a sister who died before I was born. I'm twenty-three and will marry next summer . . ."

"You got a beau?" Vivian sat up.

"Why, yes."

Vivian moved from Elizabeth's side, questions in her eyes.

"What's wrong? Come lie down. It's freezing." Elizabeth patted the sheets beside her.

"No . . . no, I don't think I should."

"And why not, for heaven's sake? Come here, I say." Elizabeth reached for her.

Vivian let herself be drawn into Elizabeth's arms. Her voice was strained. "Somehow I didn't expect to hear you were going to be married. Never even thought of it."

"Well, I'm certainly old enough."

"You just never spoke of a beau. It seems strange that a girl about to be married wouldn't speak of her beau."

"I can explain that easily enough. It's because this life out here is so new to me. I see so many things to talk of, to learn about. I can't do that if I speak only of Jonathan. Frankly, I can't stand it when the girls back home talk of nothing but their intended, as if nothing on earth existed except that one man. I find it rather boring to listen to them."

"Just seems strange you not speaking of him at all."

"Perhaps it is. But there are other things in my life right now. My memories from this time must last me forever. If I spend it pining over Jonathan, I'll miss a great deal. I don't want to do that. I write him frequently . . ."

Vivian turned from Elizabeth.

Annoyed, Elizabeth said, "A moment ago, we were the best of friends, and now you behave as if I've said something terribly wrong. What is it?"

Vivian kept her back to Elizabeth for some time and then surprised her by responding with great warmth, again drawing Elizabeth close to her. "I get ornery sometimes. It comes and goes. Think nothing of it."

She was her old self again, but Elizabeth did not understand why her mentioning her coming marriage should surprise Vivian so.

91

"What else is there to know about you?" Vivian asked.

"I graduated from finishing school, and at seventeen had a coming-out party to present me to society. There I met dozens of handsome young men, none of whom really interested me."

"Seems like a terrible waste of money just to meet a man," Vivian commented. "I met Tom at a turkey shoot and greased pig contest."

Elizabeth didn't mean to laugh, but Vivian's words were more than she could handle. She fought for control and began to choke with loud peals of laughter. She finally managed to say, "Oh, Vivian, I think I love you very much."

"Don't see what's so funny," Vivian answered sullenly. "Tom shot the turkey and caught the pig, and we had a fine feast the next day. Seems a practical way to take up with somebody, if you ask me."

"It is, darling," Elizabeth said, still laughing. "But don't you see? You and I are so different. I wish I could make you laugh when I tell you about my life. It seems so drab next to yours."

"That's why I ain't laughing."

Elizabeth laughed again.

"And unless you love a body," Vivian said seriously, "you shouldn't be telling them so."

"But I do love you, Vivian. You mean a great deal to me. And, you old grump, you can't stop me from loving you."

"Should I make you love me more?"

"Certainly. Love is a wonderful thing."

"It'll make you miss me something awful when you leave. You are still set on leaving, ain't you?"

"Yes, Vivian, dear," Elizabeth said, pinching her cheek. "I will be leaving. And, yes, I shall miss you. But I will write to you all the time. And you are coming to my wedding."

"Sheep don't allow woolies to go to weddings so far away. And not to rich city folks' weddings, especially."

"Oh, pooh, we'll find a way."

"Elizabeth," Vivian said. She spoke hesitantly, slowly. "I . . . I love you, too." Vivian turned red and buried her face against Elizabeth, muttering, "Haven't said those words in years and years."

"It's all right to love someone, Vivian," Elizabeth whispered. She stroked Vivian's hair. "It's a lovely feeling."

"It hurts."

"Oh, it does not."

"Does too."

"Not."

"Too."

They began to laugh and to tickle one another, but when Elizabeth glanced into Vivian's eyes, she saw tears, and she didn't understand what the tears were for, for Vivian wasn't laughing very hard.

Chapter 7

The first snowflake that fell from the iron-gray sky glistened in the muted light. Exquisite in design, its six white points were decorated with almost perfect precision, each delicate stem beginning with a fine point at the tip, widening in the middle and then tapering to a sheer stalk to meet at the flake's hub.

The snowflake was immediately joined by a second and then a third, and in moments the air was filled with thousands of them, each beautiful, each original, peacefully floating to the earth.

Then without warning, mighty blasts of wind

roared across the prairie, whipping the snowflakes helter-skelter, heedless of their fragile structure, smashing them to bits. Hour upon hour, thousands and then millions of flakes clogged the air with chaotic disorder, while the day lengthened into evening, and evening into night.

A single thing of beauty had now become a menace, creating hazardous drifts against Elizabeth Reynolds' small sod house as it bravely endured the brutal tempest. The winds roared down on the building, shaking the roof and madly beating against its sides, driving icy blasts of snow through walls Elizabeth had once thought so secure.

Sick with fright, Elizabeth sat huddled before the fire, remembering back to only two days ago. How nice the day had warmed as she and Vivian had ridden further and further from winter camp. But Vivian hadn't trusted the weather, and as the sun rose over the horizon they had already traveled a couple of miles.

There were no leg-stretching walks and hour-long noonings as there had been on the way to camp. They had pushed hard all that day, slept like logs on the ground that night, and continued their journey early yesterday. Vivian was determined to get home soon enough to allow Elizabeth time to make the Box R before nightfall.

Elizabeth had wanted to stay with Vivian last night and leave this morning. She had been dead tired, worn out. But Vivian had given her an emphatic "No!" There was no time left. In fifteen minutes, Elizabeth had changed her clothes, hugged her host, kissed her warmly on the cheek and then turned Billy and buggy toward home.

Her intentions had been good. She had started to the Box R. If only she hadn't been so bone weary, so exhausted, she wouldn't have fallen asleep. Three different times she had drifted off, lurching awake to find Billy, head drooping, stoically standing in the middle of the road. She had finally given up trying to reach the ranch, still twenty miles away, and stopped at the soddy for the night.

After turning the gelding into the barn, she had wasted little time building a fire and crawling beneath the bed covers. She had slept as if dead until noon today, not hearing the winds pound the soddy and howl in protest at objects impeding its insane progress. She had groggily awakened and looked through the window at a world completely wiped out by a slate-colored canvas of swirling snow.

Even though the soddy was built with foot-thick walls, the blustery gale was more than the stove could handle. According to Vivian and Polly, a sod house was never cold. Apparently this building was just too old, had seen too many storms, had been uncared for for too long.

To stay warm enough, Elizabeth wore all that she had brought with her: two pairs of wool socks, a petticoat, two dresses, and a scarf tied tightly around her head. She also wore the boots and sheepskin coat Vivian had given her, and a blanket over her lap. She wished she had kept Tom Blake's pants.

She set aside the blanket and added a few more coals to the fire. She wondered where Uncle Andy was, or one of his ranch hands. Why hadn't they ridden out to see about her? To save her? Where was Vivian? But of course, Vivian wouldn't come. She thought Elizabeth was at the ranch. And Andy probably assumed that Elizabeth was smart enough to stay with Vivian. She wasn't smart at all. She had behaved abominably, listening to no one, heeding no advice whatsoever. So she was alone. She would have to be smart now, and cautious, and she would have to *think*.

Her days of complete independence were over. Andy and Polly would get no more arguments from her about that. She didn't *want* to be independent any longer. Let someone else take care of her from now on. But it wouldn't happen before tomorrow morning, if then. No one could possibly make it through such a storm.

Head in her hands, Elizabeth whispered, "Vivian, Vivian, you are always so wise. I wish you were here. I wish you were holding me and making all the fear go away."

Again her heart welled up with terror, and she sat up and shook her head. She looked at her watch. It was late. She would go to bed. There was no sense sitting here worrying. She could lie down and worry just as well. She wrested her boots from her thick-stockinged feet and then lay down without undressing and turned out the lamp. She pulled the covers over her face, leaving only her nose and mouth exposed. Taking a deep breath, she listened to the wind roar around her, occasionally feeling snow that had found its way through unseen cracks sift onto her face.

Elizabeth dozed fitfully throughout the night, waking to a dull light in the soddy and the nerve-racking sounds of the continuing storm. She wouldn't be leaving today, and no one would be coming. She mulled over this appalling fact until she could breathe normally, then dragged herself out of bed to face a cold, dank room.

She lit a lantern and threw coal on the near-dead fire, dreading what she must do next. No matter how bad the storm, she must see to Billy. Without care since yesterday morning, he had to be ravenous. She looked out the window to see what she would be facing. After yesterday's weather, today's could only be better.

Frost had grown so thick on the pane that she first had to hold a palm against the glass to make a peephole. Peering through the small opening, she swallowed hard and felt her mouth go dry. She couldn't see five feet in front of her. Her stomach shriveled into a cold little knot, and she wanted to crawl beneath the bed covers and not confront this terrible world. But such a coward's luxury was unthinkable. Billy was her way out of here.

Still fully clothed, she had only to draw on gloves. She pushed on the door, finding some resistance, but when she tried again, the door gave. Outside, the wind nearly knocked her over before she adjusted to its direction. Shielding her eyes against its maniacal fury, she glanced down at the earth and found herself standing in two feet of snow. The drift, formed by winds whipping around the corner of the house, was half the height of the building, sloping downward to the door. Elizabeth made a mental note to bring a shovel from the barn. She must be sure to keep the entrance clear.

She walked around the side of the house, leaning

into the wind. In vain, she looked toward the barn through snow so thick that she might as well have been trying to see through a jar of milk. She thought of turning back, but guilt hit her instantly. Billy needed her care as much as she would need his when this was over.

She guessed at about where the barn might be and headed in that direction. Her eyes watered from the frigid temperatures, and she could feel her lashes sticking together as icy blasts of wind threatened to freeze her eyelids completely shut. She held a hand before her face to ward off the onslaught of tiny pellets of ice that sanded her face raw in seconds. Her breath was sucked from her lungs, stinging them until they burned like fire. She closed her mouth and breathed through her nose, only to have her nostrils congeal, forcing her mouth open again. The wind pierced her clothing, and balls of snow collected on the bottoms of her skirts and petticoat, weighing her down.

Only a few feet from the house, she was already hip-deep in snow and sweating with exertion. She glanced back frequently to keep her bearings, using the soddy for guidance until it was hidden by the storm. She fought thick, high drifts for ten minutes, certain she was near the barn by now.

She felt resistance and stuck out a hand in front of her. The pump! She was only ten yards from the house! She had not been traveling in a straight line at all, but in a wide circle. Unbelieving, she was stupefied with shock. How could she have been so lost in such a small amount of space?

Clinging to the pump, she frantically wondered what to do. She couldn't just stand here until she froze to death. She must move. She must get back to the house and start over. She felt the pump and by its shape was able to determine that the soddy was to her left, the direction the nozzle faced. She stood directly in front of it and began to walk forward, praying that she was traveling in a straight line.

Five minutes passed before she saw the house, looming only a few yards in front of her. Before entering, she kicked snow away from the door, dismayed to see that more had visibly collected during the short time she had been away.

Inside, the soddy felt warm, and she sank onto the bed; out of breath, scared, she wondered how she was going to take care of Billy.

She rested for twenty minutes before making a second attempt to reach the barn. More frightened than before, she had to push even harder on the door to get out this time. The snow was coming down faster than ever.

Fighting the blizzard again, and no longer believing it just a passing storm, Elizabeth momentarily bolstered her courage by thinking of how brave she was. A powerful gust knocked her sideways teaching her an instant lesson. Nothing must be allowed to distract her. She must concentrate only on the barn's direction.

She clawed her way over the deeper drifts, some reaching to her shoulders. She was so tired that she wanted only to sink down into the snow and rest. But she knew the dangers of such folly and drove herself to go forward.

Ten minutes later, she had not yet reached her destination. But she was *positive* she had correctly kept her bearings. She struggled for another five minutes, no longer sure where she was, only certain that she was further than ever from the barn. Then, like a beacon in the night she heard Billy whistle over the high-pitched noise of the wind. "Oh, thank God," she cried. Her words were torn from her throat and cast aside along with the snowflakes tearing by.

Following Billy's whinnies, she scrambled clumsily across the uneven snow, tumbling from the top of a high drift and rolling to a stop against the corral. She grabbed the top rail and dragged herself up, trembling and scraping snow from her eyes. She stayed with the fence, following it hand over hand to the barn as the storm unmercifully hammered her. She found the door, pushed it open, and fell inside.

She rested where she lay, breathing deeply of dirt and manure and pulverized hay. Billy continued to call and to prance. Twice she heard him kick the stall. His desperate need of food and drink drove her to her feet. It took all the energy she had to push herself to clean the stall and to pour grain into his feed bucket.

With a shovel, she brought in snow and filled his trough. She prayed the snow would not freeze, knowing she could not possibly draw water from the pump. She would never be able to carry a bucket that far. And she might miss the barn entirely . . . as she had done once already. She added more snow to the trough until it formed a formidable mound and then turned to face the storm again.

While traveling toward the barn, she'd noticed that the wind had kept striking her right side. Using this bit of information now, she kept the wind to her left, hoping this orientation would guide her safely back to the house.

The blizzard pushed and pulled at her until she was sure she had been wrong about the wind's direction. Perhaps it had only seemed like it had struck her right side. Maybe it had been her back . . . or her front. She could no longer remember. She was about to turn to the left and try that way when again she bumped into the pump. She sank to her knees, sobbing in overwhelming relief. Once more she used the nozzle to orient herself and, in minutes, made it back to the cabin.

She walked over to the coal pile, wondering in a dazed way why she hadn't thought to bring the shovel from the barn. She pushed the thought from her as too great to think about right now and began to dig through the snow to the black fuel beneath. The coal had frozen together, and she had to kick chunks loose before flinging them toward the door. Halfway through her job, she was too tired to continue and gave up the notion of bringing in even one more chunk. Only half of what she wanted sat just inside the soddy door when she pulled it shut behind her. And she had been too tired to kick the door free of snow. She would rest first and then she would tackle the coal and snow again.

She was so cold that she overfilled the stove, so hungry that she ate too much. But in an hour's time she felt better and was glad that she had played the glutton. She lay down and slept away her exhaustion.

She woke late in the afternoon, finding that snow had visibly sifted through the walls and onto the bed and shelves. The soddy was cold, and the fire had died. She scrambled to relight it, using cats to stoke the coal.

She ate and continued feeding the flames, spending the rest of the day before the stove, getting up from time to time to stretch her legs. She ate again and tried to read, an impossible task with the wind noisily battering itself against the walls and rattling the thin pane of glass.

The day slid slowly by without letup from the blizzard, and by evening Elizabeth decided she must fetch more coal. She mentally fortified herself for the short time she would have to be outdoors and pushed on the door. As before, it resisted her efforts and she tried again. Still the door did not move. A sick feeling engulfed her, and she nearly collapsed in panic, knowing without seeing that the door was blocked by the drift that had been growing since this morning. She forced herself not to cry, wishing uselessly that Vivian were here. Vivian would know what to do. Vivian always knew what to do.

Elizabeth made a desperate lunge against the door, grunting tearfully with the effort. Fifteen minutes of beating herself against it had not moved it an inch. She was trapped inside. "Please, God," she desperately prayed, "help me out of this terrible dilemma."

Exhausted from strenuous effort, she sat down to collect herself. She would allow herself only fifteen minutes of rest and then she would try again.

She awoke with a start, noticing a chill in the air. She must have been asleep for hours. Frantically, she lighted a lantern, then threw open the stove door. The coals were almost dead, and the night was hard upon her.

Hurriedly, she rebuilt the fire. Blessedly relieved

by its growing flames, she lighted every lantern and set them around the soddy, giving the place a false sense of warmth and security.

She opened a can of peaches and set it on top of the stove to take the chill off the fruit. The heat ignited the paper on the can, turning it brown and then black. Sitting in front of the stove and protected with a glove, she held the hot can in one hand and ate the sweet fruit. The food was good, and she ate guiltily, thinking of Billy with probably little left in his stall to eat. Unable to help him, she forced him from her mind.

She estimated that she had enough coal to get through the night and most of the next day if she was very, very careful. But by then she must get out.

Knowing she should not sleep, she fought throughout the night to stay awake by reading, walking around, and singing to herself. And slowly and stingily, she fed the stove. Each passing hour left her eyes more leaden. The cold of the cabin and the wisps of wind through the cracks whittled away at her reserves. By then, she barely noticed the smell of the chamberpot.

On the second day, she cried as she again rammed and battered herself over and over against the door which would not budge an inch. she thought of smashing the window and climbing out, but the problem of resealing it seemed as great as opening the door.

She waited yet another day for the storm to subside, not having slept for two nights, not having dared to sleep. "Hell," she cursed uncharacteristically, "I can survive a little snowstorm." She whirled and screamed at the door, "And Billy, you'd damn well better, too!"

The third day passed while Elizabeth watched the coal dwindle to almost nothing. She calculated that it would last halfway through the night. After that she would tear her bed apart and feed its wooden frame into the stove a piece at a time.

Bolstered by a newly discovered fuel supply, she fried some bacon and potatoes and sat wolfing her food by her tiny fire. The food made her groggy, and very early the following morning, lulled by the monotonous sound of the wind, exhausted from worry and lack of sleep, she fell into a deep slumber, her chin resting against her chest and her mind desperately trying to keep her alert.

Chapter 8

"Oh dear, oh dear, oh dear," the tiresome voice persistently repeated. Wanting only to sleep, Elizabeth tried unsuccessfully to shut out the piercing, frantic words.

Someone was pushing her around, hauling her to somewhere. Layer by layer something heavy descended upon her until she felt trapped and claustrophobic. She began to thrash about fighting against the weight. A hand caressed her cheek, soothing her quiet. Again she heard the voice: "Oh dear, oh dear."

At last there was silence, and she slept restlessly,

her dreams filled with nightmares. Once she woke and struggled to rise. It was time to feed the fire. But her body felt leaden, bound by tons of rock. She gave in to the oppressive weight and slept again.

She drifted lazily upward through a gray haze, as something brushed against her cheeks and eyes. Her thoughts sluggishly rose from the depths of exhaustion as she became more and more conscious of her surroundings.

Her first awareness was that the soddy finally was warm and filled with delicious aromas of boiling meat and onions. She swallowed, her mouth salivating. And there was this frequent softness against her face.

She opened her eyes to see Vivian sitting on the bed beside her. Vivian leaned forward and kissed her on the forehead. "Oh, Elizabeth," she whispered. "Your fire was dead. You were so cold, so cold. But you're going to be all right. Oh, my dear, you'll be fine now." She softly kissed Elizabeth's cheeks and eyes, brushing Elizabeth's lips with her own.

Elizabeth pushed back thick layers of covers and reached for Vivian. "Thank God you came," she whispered. Tears filled her eyes as she encircled Vivian with her arms. The last bit of grogginess left her, and she felt protected and loved and wanted. She gazed into Vivian's eyes. "I don't know what I would do without you. I just don't know." Then in a rush, she started to sit up. "Billy!"

"He's fine," Vivian said, gently pushing her back down. "He's hungrier than he's used to, but he'll be all right."

For a long time the two women did nothing more than look at each other, Elizabeth intensely studying Vivian's face, memorizing the planes of her cheeks, her forehead, her chin, the tilt of her nose. Inside, she felt herself grow to the size of a mountain, the moment swelling with awakening sensations she had never known before.

She placed both hands on Vivian's cheeks and felt herself magnetically drawn upward toward her. There was no pulling back, no pausing . . . no questioning the intimacy of the moment. Her lips met Vivian's in a lover's kiss.

They kissed again, this time Vivian's kiss, thunderous, wild, charged with heat. In reply, Elizabeth clung hard against her. Vivian shifted her weight so that she lay beside Elizabeth and then shifted again to lie on top of her, burying her face in Elizabeth's hair.

Elizabeth freed the bun that Vivian wore, her hair falling in tickling silken strands over their faces.

Vivian set Elizabeth on fire as her tongue — so soft, moist — touched her own.

Vivian's breath came in a great rush. She pressed down upon Elizabeth, kissing her eyes, her mouth and then moving lower down to her throat until heavy layers of clothing stopped her. Raising herself on one elbow, she put a hand on the center of Elizabeth's chest, holding it there, palm flat, fingers spread wide. Her eyes were shut, her head tilted slightly back, nostrils flaring with each deep breath she took. She stayed that way and Elizabeth pushed Vivian's hair away from her face, only to have it tumble forward again.

Elizabeth breathed deeply and attempted to slow herself down, to gather herself. Gradually, she became more steady, the powerful turbulence of the moment passing.

Vivian rolled to one side and then swung her feet off the bed. She heaved a great shudder and sat quietly for some time before asking, "Do you want to eat?"

Elizabeth refrained from reaching for Vivian, glad Vivian did not start questioning their actions. "Please."

Using pillows for back support, Elizabeth stayed in bed and dug into the stew Vivian handed her. "You can't imagine how good this tastes," she said.

Vivian filled a second bowl for herself and drew a chair alongside the bed. "We should talk when you're up to it."

Elizabeth smiled slightly. "I don't seem to be unfit." If anything, she felt as if she could lick a herd of buffalo — a cowboy's way of thinking after kissing his first girl, she suspected.

"You let me down real bad," Vivian said.

Elizabeth's spoon paused midway to her mouth. After the way they had just spent their last five minutes together, she hadn't expected Vivian to begin this way. She put down the spoon and placed her hand on Vivian's knee. "I'm so sorry, Vivian. I meant to leave. I just delayed too long."

"I told you to go straight home."

Like a living thing, shame crawled up Elizabeth's neck.

"Out here when we make a promise, we keep it." Vivian ate steadily, talking around her food, her voice controlled. "Andy and Polly are sick with fear, wondering if you're dead or alive."

"You've been to the Box R? But why are you here, and not Andy?"

"I acted like a fool, too. I should have stayed

109

where I was, but I went to the Box R to see you the day after you left. When Andy saw you weren't with me, we both started out for here. The blizzard hit so hard it blinded us. Andy's horse stumbled over something and fell on him." Vivian looked steadily at Elizabeth. "The horse busted Andy's leg."

"Oh, my God," Elizabeth whispered. She set aside her bowl and leaned her head against her knees. "It's my fault. He's hurt because of me."

"So we had to turn back," Vivian continued in a passionless voice. "We almost didn't make it. Andy's real mad, Elizabeth — at me, and at you."

"Why at you?"

"He thinks I should have been able to convince you to go home."

"You tried, as I recall."

Vivian placed her empty bowl on the table. "Andy let me use his sleigh, but I couldn't leave before last night. It's a damn good thing the weather broke and I thought to throw a shovel into the sleigh or you'd be dead as frozen coyote bait right now."

"Lord, I thought I was going to go back to New York with some wonderful stories about my life out here," Elizabeth said. "So far I've been totally irresponsible. Who would want to admit to that kind of behavior?"

Noncommittally, Vivian shrugged. "Anyway," she finished, "you're going home tomorrow — providing the weather holds long enough."

"I'd rather go to your ranch with you," Elizabeth answered.

Leaning toward her, Vivian coldly replied, "Listen to me, woman. I don't trust that weather out there for one damn minute. My sheep ain't seen me in four days, and I got to get home. Your family needs you now, and I can't be taking care of someone who's supposed to already know how to take care of herself."

"Look, Vivian," Elizabeth began. "I know I'm responsible for this whole mess. But Andy has Polly to look after him, so I can go back to the ranch and idly sit and rock the days away, or I can make myself useful at Sheephaven. I didn't do that badly here until I got blocked in."

"Are you loco?" Vivian shouted at her. "You damn near died!" The smaller, yet more powerful woman reached out and grabbed Elizabeth, shaking her as if she were a sack of rags. "You ought to be whipped."

Surprised by her vehemence, Elizabeth pulled Vivian's hands from her. "All right, I was stupid and I'm sorry. But let me fix things. Let me *do* something to make amends."

"Hell, Elizabeth, you can't make amends on my ranch. What you'd have to do would kill most women and exhaust most men. You'd just get in my way — and I won't have it. You're going home."

Dazed by Vivian's anger, Elizabeth wondered what had happened to the magic they had shared only minutes ago.

An uneasy peace fell over the soddy, and the women talked little for the remainder of the day. That night, they slept locked in each other's arms, but Elizabeth did not try to kiss Vivian. It was not a time for kissing. This caring woman was infuriated with Elizabeth, and Elizabeth knew it.

Before first light, they ate a hearty breakfast, and thickly bundled against the raw wind and low temperature, they were soon skimming across the prairie. They rode gracefully along the tall sculpted drifts, the driving team rhythmically snorting billowing clouds of steam. Tied to the hitch by a lead rope, Billy followed behind. Elizabeth watched the sun rise, casting long rays of yellow light across the land.

"It must be forty below," Vivian commented.

Elizabeth didn't care what the temperature was. She only cared that they were headed toward the Box R instead of Sheephaven. She replied, "So help me, Vivian, as soon as you take me back, I'll follow you — on foot if need be, but I will be with you. I . . . I belong there."

"Like hell."

"I belong there!"

"Damn it, Elizabeth. What about Andy with his busted leg, and Polly with all those chores? She's got chickens and a goat and two milk cows to tend to."

"They have eight hired hands on that ranch, Vivian. Aunt Polly doesn't have to do anything except to feed Andy."

"Them hands will be out with the cattle. Your folks need you, Elizabeth."

"And I need *you*, Vivian."

Vivian pulled the sleigh to a halt. She turned to face Elizabeth. "Is this about yesterday . . . about last night?"

"It is."

"You got a beau."

Vivian glared at Elizabeth, piercing her soul. Elizabeth dropped her eyes, intently studying her mitted hands. She did not want to hear about Jonathan.

"You got a beau," Vivian repeated.

Elizabeth ignored Vivian's words, taking her in her arms. She pressed her mouth against Vivian's, not knowing if she would be rejected. Vivian did not pull away, and Elizabeth kissed her with great longing and desire. She nuzzled her way between Vivian's thick collar and the warm skin protected beneath. Gently, she bit Vivian, kissed the spot and then kissed her on the lips, searching the inside of her mouth with her tongue. Vivian responded passionately, holding Elizabeth tightly and never saying a word.

"I need you, Vivian," Elizabeth whispered. "I will follow you." When Elizabeth released her, Vivian took up the reins and began to drive as if the moment had not occurred. She spoke little for the remainder of the trip.

It took them two hours to reach the ranch, and as soon as Elizabeth shouted to the house, Polly stumbled out through four-foot drifts to greet her, openly weeping in grateful relief. She grasped Elizabeth to her, fawning over her and dragging her inside to the warm kitchen. There Andy sat, heavily scowling, his splinted leg propped on a stool before the stove.

He spoke in a loud, wrathful voice. "Elizabeth Reynolds, I ought to send you back to New York right now, except I don't want your father to know what a fool you've made of your Aunt Polly and me — and what a fool you are."

Elizabeth sank beside her uncle, wrapping her arms around his neck. "I'm sorry, Uncle Andy. I'm so sorry. I don't know what to say."

"You better start listening to someone, girl," he answered angrily. "Being thoughtless in Montana Territory can kill you."

And it almost had. Elizabeth glanced at Vivian, willing her not to say a word about how Vivian had found her. But Vivian remained silent.

Polly took Elizabeth by the shoulders and drew her to her feet. "Come, dear, take off your coat. Have something to eat. Vivian, eat something before you go home."

"I must see to the horses, Aunt Polly," Elizabeth said.

Vivian started for the door. "I'll do it."

Elizabeth's commanding voice stopped her. "I insist." Vivian had already done enough.

As she drove the sleigh toward the barn, Elizabeth envisioned herself struggling on foot through the snow, following Vivian, calling after her as she rode away, dramatically reaching out with one hand while supporting herself upright where she had fallen, with the other.

"I would not only look ridiculous, but it would be a ridiculous act," she said aloud.

She took care of the horses, beginning with Billy. "There you are, Billy boy," she said. "I hope you're not mad at me, too."

The gelding nuzzled her, and she leaned her face against his thick winter coat and tangled her fingers in his mane, already feeling the pain of missing Vivian. "I wish I were stronger, Billy. I wish I could go with her. And I wish I could do without her."

Again she saw herself trailing on foot after Vivian,

helplessly calling her name. She stood straight. "You've got to stop reading trash, Elizabeth. Things like that just don't happen."

She returned to the house, knowing with an aching heart that it might be weeks, perhaps months, before she saw Vivian again.

All three sat waiting at the table. Obviously still provoked, Andy asked, "Figure out which strap went where?"

Elizabeth struggled to keep her voice pleasant as she hung up her coat and hat. Forcing herself to smile, she replied, "I grained them all and rubbed them down."

Grudgingly, he answered, "Good girl," still scowling deeply at her.

"Sit down, Elizabeth," Polly urged. "Pay those two no mind. They think that anyone who can't do all they can isn't worth half his salt. Yes, I'm talking about you, too, Vivian Blake," she said, shaking a scolding finger at Vivian's raised eyebrows. "I'm just thankful the three of you are all right." She filled their plates with beefsteak, potatoes, and gravy. "There's plenty more, so don't be shy."

The conversation centered around the storm and the expected cattle and sheep losses for the ranchers and how lucky Elizabeth was that Vivian got her safely home.

Finished with her meal, Vivian stood and reached for her wraps. "I'd better be going."

"Thank you for bringing my niece back," Andy told her. He shook Vivian's hand, which surprised and pleased Elizabeth.

"No trouble," Vivian answered.

As she and Vivian headed for the barn, Elizabeth said, "You lied to Andy. I was nothing but trouble."

"Forget it," Vivian said. "It's over." Then she asked, "Are you out here to trail after me?"

"No, my place is here for now," Elizabeth conceded. "But will you let me kiss you goodbye?"

Vivian nodded, and as soon as they entered the barn Elizabeth pulled the door shut behind them and took Vivian in her arms. They kissed long and deep and came up gasping for air. Elizabeth felt unsteady on her feet. "When will I see you again?"

Vivian leaned heavily against her. "I don't know. The weather's bound to get bad again."

"Will you miss me?"

"I'll miss you. But I'll adjust. And you should, too. This is just plain foolishness."

"It *isn't* foolishness, Vivian. What I feel for you is real."

"Real? How can it be real? You'll be leaving come summer, Elizabeth."

"And until then? Why can't we have what we have? I don't want to be separated from you."

"What good will it do us?"

"What harm?"

"None now, maybe. It's the thought of parting later on that I can't handle. I can hardly handle it now."

"It's not that serious for us."

"God, Elizabeth, it's that serious. I can't think for want of you. I got feelings. Strong feelings." Vivian's voice became low, husky.

She walked to a ladder leading to the loft and stood quietly at its foot, her hand resting on a rung.

Elizabeth walked over to her, her heart beating out of control, her mind only half aware of where she was, what she was doing.

They climbed to the loft and lay down side by side on the hay piled there. Neither spoke, as Elizabeth watched Vivian's breath turn to mist and fill the space between them.

Elizabeth whispered, "You laid on top of me at the soddy. Will you do it again?"

"Yes."

Vivian was light, seeming to weigh nothing at all as she rested full-length on Elizabeth. They began to kiss, Elizabeth's body already burning. She spread her legs and Vivian nestled within. As her lips covered Vivian's, Elizabeth felt a rising sense of power. They stopped only long enough to pull off their gloves and push away their hats, the bitter cold air nipping at their flesh as they left wet kisses upon one another.

"Vivian," Elizabeth pleaded. "Please . . . touch me."

Vivian reached beneath Elizabeth's coat and under the blouse that she wore. Her hand was warm against Elizabeth's skin as her fingers found a nipple.

Elizabeth gritted her teeth against the thrilling sensation streaking up her legs and into her belly. Again Vivian touched her, lightly moving her hand across both breasts, taking each nipple between gentle fingers, squeezing, then releasing, and squeezing again.

"I can't stand this, Vivian," Elizabeth said. The sensations were too forceful.

Vivian moved off Elizabeth and kissed her and then again sought a breast.

Elizabeth held Vivian tightly, wishing they were at

the soddy. There would have been no cumbersome clothing separating their bodies, only each other beneath the blankets. The vision of her lying nude next to Vivian renewed the heat between her legs.

Vivian slipped her hand beneath Elizabeth's petticoat, to her silken underwear.

Elizabeth murmured incoherently as Vivian positioned her hand lower, resting it on soft hair. Elizabeth drew in a sharp breath, straining for Vivian. She felt a finger touch her and a pulsing rhythm begin. Elizabeth clung wildly to Vivian, Vivian barely moving her hand, the feeling in Elizabeth growing stronger and stronger.

She floated away from earth, detached from all she had ever known, becoming a part of Vivian, being consumed by her. The pulsations continued on forever.

She could stand it no longer, and she brought her knees together, clamping them tight, Vivian's hand locked between her thighs. She dragged Vivian's hand away, the movement making her jump.

She felt trickles of sweat slide down her ribcage. The air cooled the moisture on her face.

Gazing down on her, Vivian asked, "Do we need to talk?"

"Not at all." With her body half resting on Vivian, Elizabeth tried to repeat what Vivian had done, feeling clumsy and inadequate. Vivian reassured her, and Elizabeth cupped Vivian's breast with her hand. It surprised Elizabeth that Vivian was so small. But Vivian was different, in every way — different.

Elizabeth closed her eyes, envisioning how her

hand looked resting against Vivian's flesh. The image started the blood pounding in her ears.

They kissed and whispered each other's name over and over. Vivian reached beneath Elizabeth's blouse and put both hands on her bare back. "You are a lady, my love," she whispered.

"And so are you," Elizabeth replied huskily, her lips pressed lightly against Vivian's as she spoke.

She touched Vivian's nipples and imagined taking one into her mouth. She would, one day. They would lay nude together in a beautiful field of thick, green grass, and she would suck softly on Vivian. She cradled Vivian in her arms as her hand slipped beneath her pants. She could feel the multiple buttons of long underwear and smiled against Vivian's cheek. She kissed her tenderly and knew that she loved this woman deeply.

Coarse hair caressed Elizabeth's hand. She molded her palm to Vivian's shape as Vivian grasped her tightly to her body. Slowly, Elizabeth slipped her fingers into the inner depths of Vivian, the wetness like an ocean of love. Vivian's legs fell wide and inviting. "You are beautiful," Elizabeth whispered.

Vivian's breathing was audible, each breath a force of air becoming more and more rapid until her final breath was a great gasp and then a single long sigh. She lay still, Elizabeth remaining within her.

Elizabeth withdrew and reached up to stroke Vivian's hair. She could smell Vivian on her skin. The odor was intoxicating. She moved on top of Vivian, ready, unable to think, able only to feel.

She heard Vivian's voice but could not

119

comprehend her words. Vivian spoke again against the smear of Elizabeth's impassioned kisses. "I must go, Elizabeth. Stop. I must go."

Elizabeth finally understood what she was saying. But Vivian couldn't leave her. Not now. "Stay tonight," she begged, and began to kiss Vivian again.

"Elizabeth, stop."

Her compelling tone brought Elizabeth to her senses. She slowly moved to one side and sat up. "Yes, yes, I'm sorry. No, I'm not sorry . . . except that you must go."

Vivian began to pick hay from Elizabeth's hair. "I would rather stay, Elizabeth. You know I would."

Elizabeth pressed Vivian's hand to her lips. "I know." She felt the thick, rough callouses. How was she to face a single day without this woman?

They climbed from the loft and straightened their clothing, making sure no hay clung to either of them.

"Kiss me goodbye, Elizabeth," Vivian said, "and then I'll be able to make it home all right."

They kissed and cried and wiped away each other's tears.

Vivian saddled her horse quickly and Elizabeth followed her outside. Once mounted, Vivian turned and said, "If I could, I'd play like one of those knights in shining armor and sweep you off your feet and clean away from here."

Smiling, Elizabeth replied, "I had a similar fantasy earlier today and then decided it would be impractical."

"Some dreams are. But then some dreams aren't."

Vivian tipped her hat and nudged her horse in the flanks.

Tears freezing on her cheeks, Elizabeth watched

her until she was hidden from sight by a towering drift.

And never was Jonathan further from her thoughts than he was right now.

Chapter 9

Days turned into weeks and weeks into months, and the weather became a creature gone berserk, screaming down from distant peaks, scouring the earth clean where mountain met prairie and covering the rest of Montana beneath a thick blanket of snow. Three fierce blizzards struck between November and January. Endless snowstorms, each hardly distinguishable from the blizzards, blasted the land. Freak thaws glazed the snow, building a crust so thick that it could withstand the weight of horse and man. Drifts nearly buried soddies and barns and concealed watering holes. Snow filled the gullies level with the land, making it impossible for cattle to find protection from winter's merciless rage.

While Elizabeth worried constantly about Vivian, knowing she was out in this terrible weather, Andy sat healing in the house. As restless as the winds that blew, he grumbled at the women.

By mid-December he was back on his feet and began to venture out daily with his men, searching for his cattle. He left before dawn and was back by nightfall, shivering from head to toe, his beard and moustache caked with ice, his eyes glassy and red-rimmed. Stomping and peeling off his wraps before the fire, he shed huge clods of snow before the fire. And he always returned with the same report: "I've seen hundreds of dead cattle piled against buildings, against fences, stacked in draws. The wind just keeps driving 'em south. And that isn't the end of it. The ground's so froze over, those that are still alive can't eat because they can't break through the ice covering. Every damn one of them is starving." He talked with a slur, his lips still gripped by the cold. He limped from pain and stiffness in his leg but spoke only of the terrible plight of his herd. "This is the end of the open range, Polly," he told her. "You watch and see." Polly and Elizabeth turned away from his tears.

Once, Elizabeth went out with him to search for cattle. Even though she empathized with Andy's grief, she also wanted to know what Vivian was feeling when she was out with her sheep. If she couldn't be with Vivian, she wanted to at least share her discomfort.

The day she chose to go was warm, the sky a

brilliant blue, the air still and clear. She rode beside her uncle, both of them heavily bundled as insurance against an unpredictable change in the weather.

They traveled for miles before finding their first cow. She stood straddle-legged on the ice crust, blood dripping from deep lacerations criss-crossing her nose where she had repeatedly tried to break through the tough four-inch layer. A large crimson color stained the snow beneath her long face. Elizabeth could count the bovine's ribs and imagined she saw tears in the animal's eyes. It looked helplessly at her, bawling pathetically in its last stages of starvation. Andy pulled out his revolver and pointed it at her head. "Don't look," he said, but Elizabeth did, and at the crack of the pistol she saw the cow jump and then crumple, the light quickly fading from its eyes. Elizabeth looked at her uncle, who sat rigid in the saddle. Openly crying, he said, "Damned old cow wasn't good for nothin' anyway."

Elizabeth didn't go with him again.

She spent hours in the kitchen with Polly, learning to cook every meal her aunt had ever prepared and new ones besides, thinking that she should have known years ago how to do this. She no longer thought of tea and pastry at three in the afternoon as a midday's refreshment. It was a joke.

Together the women became inventive as the potatoes, turnips, squash, onions, and carrots stored in the shallow cellar beneath the floorboards dwindled. Even the chickens had nearly stopped laying. With reaching Billings for supplies impossible, they began to substitute molasses for sugar and to severely ration their coffee. They gave Andy all the sugar and coffee he wanted as long as the staples held out.

During the first week of February, he brought back news of several needy families, and Polly and Elizabeth went to their aid. Managing to get out about twice a week, they delivered food supplies they themselves could scarcely spare. Fighting stiff leather straps and metal buckles too cold to touch, they stopped frequently to pull off their mittens and warm their hands by the heat of a lantern before they could finish hitching the sleigh for their dangerous journeys.

Several babies, and older children as well, fell to the bitter cold seeping through walls of poorly made soddies. Others were victims of the dreaded measles. Their small bodies were wrapped in precious blankets and, to deter predators, sprinkled with lime before being buried deep in the snow near the soddies. Proper burials would take place when the chinook winds arrived. And everyone slept lightly, ready to drive off hungry wolves that occasionally came nosing around.

It wouldn't be long now, folks told each other hopefully. This was February. The chinook winds had to be coming soon. Elizabeth clung hard to this thought, expressing the same enthusiasm as did those who had lived in Montana for years. She was glad that winter was nearly over. It meant she would soon see Vivian.

She prepared many of the meals now, smiling and cooing as she held tired mothers' babies in her arms. She experienced great satisfaction whenever she helped someone else.

But at night, away from these busy affairs and alone in her bed, she ached for Vivian, and as always Jonathan entered her thoughts. Confusingly, she loved them both. But she had already shared herself with Vivian, in a way she had been taught one saved for the marriage bed. She wasn't stupid enough to think that Jonathan hadn't availed himself of the houses around New York. She knew they existed. She excused him, knowing that was the way of men — their outlet. But she excused herself, as well. Her time with Vivian had been no outlet. It had been a lovely surprise.

During the day in the house's warm kitchen, she wrote letters to Jonathan to be sent whenever the weather finally broke. But more often, as she swept the house clean or washed dishes or rolled bread dough, she lost herself in thoughts of Vivian, reliving the times when Vivian's strong arms had held her, feeling again her gentle touch, hearing once more her rare laughter.

Early one morning Elizabeth and Polly sat in the kitchen sharing their daily coffee when a heavy knock came to the door. Polly hadn't reached it before a man made his way in uninvited, quickly slamming the door behind him. He stood six feet tall, his hat nearly scraping the ceiling and his heavy clothing concealing the giant beneath. His unkempt black beard hid most of his face and his dark eyes were bright with fever.

Elizabeth had never seen him before. He looked desperate, and she backed slowly away from him. She moved toward the rifle that stood in the corner, left there for the protection of the women whenever they were alone.

"My wife and baby are terrible sick, Polly. I can't

tend them anymore." He blurted out the words and then slumped into a chair. He looked beaten and afraid. "I'm having a hell of a time trying to run the ranch and take care of them, too. I heard you and your niece there been out helping folks. Hilda asked if you might come over and help us a few days."

"Elizabeth, this is Marcus Donavan. Him and his wife, Hilda, are our neighbors to the south. Pour him some coffee." Polly quickly slapped a slice of beef into a frying pan on the stove.

Donavan nodded to Elizabeth and coughed deeply. "Damn! I can't shake this. The baby's got colic, and Hilda's in bed permanent."

Soon Polly had a heaping plate of food before him. "You take our goat," she told him. "We can spare her. Elizabeth, you pack up and go with Marcus. You'll take the sleigh. Do like Marcus tells you and you'll be fine."

"But Aunt Polly," Elizabeth began to protest. "I can't . . ." She couldn't possibly take care of a sick family all by herself! Polly had always been with her whenever she had tended people, with Polly doing most of the tending. All she had truly done was prepare some meals, change diapers, hold babies . . .

"Get ready!" Polly spoke sharply, and turned away.

Elizabeth stared at her back, feeling ashamed and helpless.

Marcus cleaned his plate and then headed for the door. With his hand on the latch, he said, "I'll be back to fetch you in ten minutes, Missy." His eyebrows, great black, bushy things, drew together in a deep scowl above the bridge of his nose. "You be ready."

Elizabeth nodded, frightened by him and terrified at the thought of this newest responsibility thrust upon her.

As soon as the door closed, Polly brandished the spatula she held like a weapon. "Don't you ever shame me in front of anybody that comes to this door again, Elizabeth Reynolds." She shook the utensil at her niece, droplets of grease sailing across the room. "Out here, if somebody asks for help, we help! It doesn't matter if we can do the job or not — we still do our best. That's the way of it. There's an extra female in this house, she's the one to take up the slack in time of need. That's you, girl. Now go and get your things. Scoot!" She slapped Elizabeth smartly on the rump as Elizabeth turned from her and scurried away.

Suddenly, Elizabeth was sick to death of Montana. She wanted to go home. Life here was too hard, too impossible. Why, she asked herself, did people purposefully punish themselves by staying in this dreadful place under such appalling conditions? She hated it here. *Hated* it! She longed to have Jonathan come and take her away. She wouldn't even have to open a door for herself. He would do it. He would do everything and care for her completely.

She didn't even know these people she was expected to help. What if she couldn't help them? What if the baby died? Worse, perhaps, what if the wife died? What would Mr. Donavan do? Would he go crazy with grief like one of her uncle's friends had when his wife died, and shoot up the place or run out into the snow until he was lost forever, like Aunt Polly had said old Bill Sallen had done when his woman died? Didn't people here just grieve properly if someone passed away and simply go to their funerals? The place was insane. The land was insane, the weather was insane. She stood twisting a sweater into a tight little knot, her anxiety almost more than she could bear.

She returned to the kitchen, a small bag in her hand. Polly bustled about, gathering a basket of things together for Elizabeth to take along. Elizabeth could tell by her actions that she was still angry. Before Elizabeth could apologize, knowing that she must, Polly said, "What if Jonathan died because you were too afraid to help him, Elizabeth? How would you feel? Or what if it was Vivian? I know how much you think of her. You follow her around like a puppy. What if she was sick? Wouldn't you want to at least try to help her?"

Even the mention of Vivian's name didn't make Elizabeth feel any better. "It just seems as if it would be wiser if you went, Aunt Polly. You know so much more than I do. It isn't like I would be taking care of myself, living alone, with only me to see to. These people are sick! They may die."

"Not if you do your job. Hilda can direct you from the bed. Marcus will help when he's there. Just let me tell you about the goat."

The goat! She had forgotten about it.

"You'll have to milk her two times a day. Morning and night. She hasn't been milked today, so you'll have to do it as soon as you get to the Donavans. Heat the milk till it simmers, then let it cool until you can stick your finger in it and it doesn't burn you. Make a nipple with a twist of cloth. Dip it in the milk and let the baby suck on that. He can't take cow's milk, and Hilda's milk won't be good while she's sick. I've sent along some sugar in case Hilda's out. Put some in the baby's milk. Let him suck on apples soaked in hot sugar water, too. Can you remember all that?"

Elizabeth nodded mutely as Polly put a firm hand on her shoulder. "Child, if I didn't think you could do this, I wouldn't send you. I'm surprised you think you can't. I could almost hate my brother for making such a helpless girl out of you. But then, that's the way rich men are with their women. They turn them into nothing but useless ornaments." She dropped her hand to her side and studied her niece's eyes, saying firmly, "When you go back to New York, you won't be helpless anymore."

"I'm not helpless, Aunt Polly."

Polly continued as if she hadn't heard. "Maybe you'll be spoiled for that life. You're going to end up not knowing what to do with yourself."

Never! thought Elizabeth. She couldn't wait to return home, to begin writing wedding invitations, visiting friends missed, going to parties and balls with Jonathan close by her side.

Marcus came in, blowing on his bare hands. "Ready, Missy?"

Polly hugged her niece. "Just mind what Marcus and Hilda tell you."

"I don't know how to milk a goat, Aunt Polly," Elizabeth whispered desperately.

"When are you bringing her back, Marcus?" Polly grabbed Elizabeth's hand and gripped a single finger. She began to squeeze using one fingertip at a time from top to bottom.

"Looks like a couple, three weeks," Marcus said.

"Milk the goat just like that," Polly said close to

Elizabeth's ear, giving Elizabeth's finger one more squeeze. "Two hands on two tits at a time, till she's empty."

Elizabeth flushed and put on her wraps.

"I'll bring back the sleigh in a day or two," Marcus said. "Thanks for your help."

What help did Aunt Polly give, Elizabeth questioned silently. It was she who was going to be taking all the responsibility.

Polly handed Elizabeth the basket. She followed Elizabeth and Marcus out the door, calling goodbye as they climbed into the sleigh. Marcus had tied the goat in the sleigh and his horse to the tailgate, choosing to use the driving team. The goat kept trying to stand on Elizabeth's lap, and she repeatedly batted it out of her way.

Even bundled as she was she thought she would freeze to death before they reached Donavan's ranch. Mr. Donavan had been silent and brooding all the way, not saying two words to her.

They arrived at the soddy just after noon. "Jump down, Missy. Go on in and rustle up some food." As soon as she had her bag in her hand, Marcus drove toward the barn. It looked like it was up to her to introduce herself.

Inside, the soddy smelled of urine and sweat, the odor almost choking her. There were no lanterns burning and only the faintest of light emitting from a bed of near-dead coals in the fireplace. The sound of a baby whimpering weakly came from her left.

"Mrs. Donavan," she called.

A feeble voice answered, "There's a lantern on the table."

Elizabeth felt her head swim. She closed her eyes

to steady herself. You must do this, Elizabeth, she told herself. You *must.*

She found the lantern and lit two more besides. The soddy was small but airtight. It looked much like Vivian's with a double bed in the corner, a drysink filled with dirty dishes opposite it. Two shelves holding dishes and utensils were built above the sink. There was a single dresser, a table, four chairs, and a cradle beside a rocker.

Carrying a lantern to Hilda's bedside, Elizabeth held it near her face so that the bedridden woman could see her. Kneeling down, she said, "I'm Elizabeth Reynolds, Polly's niece. I've come to help you." Mrs. Donavan looked wasted. Beside her lay the baby, barely able to cry. "I'll build a fire and then see to your child."

She quickly shed her coat and hat and then emptied the bucket of coal standing beside the fireplace onto the embers. She used the billows to blow the glowing coals into flames. Next, she took the tiny boy in her arms. She located fresh clothing for him and soon had him clean and dry. She felt her heart swell with grief at the pathetic little being, so thin that his skin seemed translucent.

Marcus came in carrying a bucket. "I milked nanny for you. You'll have to be doing it hereafter." He set the bucket by the door and went to kneel at his wife's side, taking her hand. "How you doing?"

"I'll be fine in a day or two," she answered weakly. He kissed her and then left — for the rest of the day, Elizabeth knew.

She wondered if Mrs. Donavan believed what she had told her husband. Elizabeth surely didn't.

In a pot hanging over the flames, Elizabeth

prepared the baby's milk according to Polly's directions. It took a long time to feed him, but he finally seemed satisfied even with the little bit that he nursed, and fell asleep in her arms. She returned him to his mother and then made a thick stew. While it simmered, she changed bedding and helped Hilda into a fresh gown.

When the stew was ready, Elizabeth brought Hilda a bowlful, but she could barely get anything down. "Try the broth, Mrs. Donavan," Elizabeth encouraged. She took the spoon from Hilda's hand and fed her herself.

When Marcus came in that evening, Elizabeth made sure there was plenty of food and hot coffee for him. While he ate at the table and Hilda slept, Elizabeth held and rocked the baby before the fire. The silence stretched long and uncomfortable for Elizabeth. Unable to stand it any longer, she asked, "Have you been in Montana long, Mr. Donavan?"

"Six years."

Elizabeth looked down at the child in her arms. "What's your son's name?"

"Mark. He's our firstborn."

"He's very handsome." To the creaking of the rocker, Elizabeth began to hum a lullaby her mother had taught her as a child.

Finally Marcus stood. "I'll be going to bed now. I'll sleep on the floor here till Hilda's better."

Apparently, Mr. Donavan had been planning on her sleeping with his wife. But he was far too sick to sleep on the floor. He needed all the proper rest he could get.

"You can't do that, Mr. Donavan. You'll never get well that way."

"Well now, I surely can."

"Mr. Donavan," Elizabeth began softly. "When I was a child and didn't feel good, my father would come into my room and say to me: 'How's my little girl?' And he taught me to answer: 'Sick abed aboard two chairs.' I see four chairs here, and with enough padding and a blanket, I could put those chairs in a row next to the fireplace, and I imagine I could sleep as comfortably as if I were in my own bed."

Truthfully, she wanted to run from here and go back to New York, but this helpless baby in her arms and a woman who could barely get out of bed, and a man who would give up his only place of comfort just for her made staying possible — and bearable.

Marcus looked thoughtfully at her. "Then if you don't mind . . ."

"I shall bring your baby to you when you call," she said.

She thought she saw tears come to his eyes, but then it could have been his fever. She lowered her eyes to the baby and began humming softly, listening to the sounds of clothing dropping to the floor and the rustling of Montana feathers bending beneath Mr. Donavan's weight.

Chapter 10

Elizabeth stayed with the Donavans for four weeks. She was constantly tired. From the time she rose well before daylight, until she fell onto the chairs late at night, the demands of this family did not let her rest. She suffered painfully from her makeshift bed, her back and hips always sore and stiff, her body longing to stretch out. She was no longer concerned that Mr. Donavan might be watching her prepare for bed. She was too tired to care.

Daily chores were overwhelming: she hauled

buckets of coal and water, washed dishes, cooked, baked, and endlessly tidied the soddy. She hated doing laundry, but each morning scrubbed the clothing with lye soap against a washboard in a tub of scalding hot water. Hilda complained about putting on a fresh nightgown every couple of days. Marcus saw no good at all in changing his long underwear so much, and grumbled loudly about it. But Elizabeth was unable to shake her own standards of wearing clean clothing and firmly told the Donavans that they would get better faster if they did, too.

But her standards cost her. In three days' time, her hands began to crack and bleed from the harsh soap and the cold outdoor temperatures. At Hilda's suggestion, she rubbed bacon fat into her rough and raw hands whenever she happened to think of it.

Milking the goat was a dreadful experience. The animal hated Elizabeth, and twice a day it butted and nipped and kicked at her. But in a few days, Elizabeth's confidence grew and the strength in her hands increased. She became more proficient, and the milk hit the bucket with a rhythmic swish . . . swish . . . swish.

She healed the Donavans through instinct and by using prairie medicine that Hilda, in a hoarse whisper, taught her. She nearly vomited when Hilda insisted that she put five drops of her own urine in Hilda's ear to stop an earache. To Elizabeth's amazement, Hilda's earache went away, but Elizabeth doubted it was due to the disgusting remedy. Later, when Hilda was able to talk more, she told Elizabeth that coal oil was good for dandruff, and eating roasted mouse would get rid of measles; swallowing nine gun pellets would cure boils; a bean thrown into a well over the left shoulder would make warts go away. Elizabeth almost laughed out loud when Hilda told her that for years her mother had carried a potato in her apron pocket to drive off rheumatism in her back.

The one remedy Elizabeth did believe in was the sassafras tea she fed the baby to help him fight off spring fever. She didn't know if the tea helped, but his sipping a few drops several times a day did seem to settle him down.

Elizabeth combed Hilda's hair daily and bathed her face and throat, talking cheerfully about whatever came to mind. Often it was of the warm weather due any day now. After the first week, Hilda began to gain in strength, paying more attention to her son, smiling at him and talking to him. Elizabeth glowed inside as she watched Hilda's slow, steady progress.

With his family beginning to mend, Marcus concentrated on his duties and his health. He was wise enough not to overwork himself, an unusual trait in a man, Elizabeth remarked one day to Hilda.

"Anything else would kill him," Hilda told her. "He would rather be doing ten times what he's doing, and it's real hard for him to hold back. But he needs to get better for all of us, and he knows this is the only way."

Mark was Elizabeth's greatest worry and care. She spent hours during the day tending him, making sure he was kept dry and clean and as well fed as possible. At night, while his parents slept, she frequently sat before the fire, rocking and crooning to him as he fretted and cried. When at last he too slept, she gently placed him between his parents and wearily made up her bed for the night.

Nearly three anxious weeks passed before he showed the first signs of improvement. One afternoon he surprised her and lustily fought the cloth sugartit she held for him. She looked keenly at him, astonished at the strength he displayed. Then, for the first time, he looked clearly into her eyes and smiled a toothless smile at her. Elizabeth's heart swelled, and she said to him, "We're going to do it, Mark. You and me. Together we're going to make you well." Her eyes filled with tears as he smiled a second time.

She could not have described how relieved she was when Hilda got out of bed to see her son fighting the sugartit. Quietly, Hilda took her baby from Elizabeth's arms and sat by the fire to finish feeding him. After that Hilda ate more, moved around more. By the beginning of the fourth week, she was nursing again, smiling often, cooing at Mark, and helping with the lighter household duties.

Then one evening, as Hilda sat in the rocker nursing her son, and Marcus sat before the fire carving a stick to slivers, he said to Elizabeth, "You'll be going home in the morning."

Elizabeth stifled her joy at his unexpected news, and instead casually asked, "Are you sure you'll be all right?" Standing at the sink, she kept her back to Marcus, barely able to peel the thin skin from the onion with her trembling hands. Her every thought turned to Vivian, whom she had had little time to think of for weeks now, and guessing how soon it might be before she could see her again. If the weather stayed as mild as it had these last few days, it wouldn't be long, she was certain.

Marcus replied, "We'll be fine. You know, Missy, if it wasn't for folks pitchin' in when we needed 'em, we'd all be goners out here a whole lot sooner than we are."

"I'm glad I could help," Elizabeth answered honestly, deeply appreciating his compliment.

She was thankful now that Polly had insisted she come. She had learned so much about others — about herself.

And she could scarcely wait to leave.

Chapter 11

For three days Elizabeth rose late, catching up on badly needed rest. She behaved no differently this morning, strolling lazily into the kitchen around eleven o'clock.

Her heart leaped to her throat at the unexpected sight of Vivian casually drinking coffee and chatting across the table with Polly. Even in front of her aunt, Elizabeth could not refrain from dropping beside Vivian and unceremoniously grabbing her around the neck. She squealed with delight. "Why didn't you tell me you were here?"

Polly answered, "She just got here. Besides, we thought you were asleep."

Vivian peeled Elizabeth's arms away. "Goodness, girl, it ain't been that long."

Elizabeth stepped back to see if Vivian meant what she said, but her eyes revealed nothing. Elizabeth was a little frightened by Vivian's nonchalant reaction. Had she forgotten her over the months?

"Here," Vivian said. "You got mail."

"You've been to Billings? How on earth did the train get through?" Elizabeth picked up several letters from the table, quickly scanning them. There were three from her parents and seven from Jonathan.

"They've been sitting in the post office since late November. There hasn't been a train through since."

Carelessly, Elizabeth tossed the letters on the table. "I'll read them later." She wanted to read Jonathan's now, but Vivian would be leaving soon enough. Too soon. "How long can you stay?" she asked.

"A few minutes," Vivian replied.

Polly rose and went to the stove. "Then have some breakfast before you go."

"I'll fix it, Aunt Polly," Elizabeth reached for a bowl from the hutch. She whipped up batter and served frycakes as big as wagon wheels, drenching them in molasses. She piled biscuits from the warming oven onto a plate and placed them in front of Vivian and then sat across from her, watching her every move.

Vivian began to eat heartily. "Good frycakes, Elizabeth. Dandy biscuits, Polly."

"A day old," Polly answered.

"Wish me and my boys could cook like this." In two bites, a biscuit disappeared.

With raised eyebrows, Polly looked toward Elizabeth. "Don't you have anything to say?"

"No," Elizabeth replied.

"Well, if you won't tell her, then I will," Polly said, puffing up with pride. "I didn't bake that biscuit, Vivian. Elizabeth did."

Vivian looked up from her plate. "Best one I ever ate."

"She'll make Jonathan a fine wife," Polly commented.

Vivian dropped her eyes, and Elizabeth wanted to sink through the floor. But she certainly couldn't shush Polly. She couldn't say a word.

With a biscuit, Vivian sopped up the molasses from her plate and popped the last bite into her mouth. "Guess I'll get along, Polly. Thanks for breakfast, Elizabeth."

Polly wrapped several more biscuits in a cloth and handed them to Vivian. "Take these along. They'll keep you from getting hungry along the way. Mind you don't crush them."

Vivian buttoned her coat and donned her hat. "They won't last that long."

Wordlessly, Elizabeth, too, dressed to go out.

"Where you going?" Vivian asked.

"Just to your horse."

"Take care of yourself, Polly," Vivian said, as she stepped out into the brisk air. Elizabeth followed, closing the door behind them. Vivian pulled on her gloves. "You needn't have come out, Elizabeth. It's

142

cold." She drew her collar around her neck and stood by her horse.

Elizabeth put her hand on Vivian's arm. "I've missed you." Vivian's eyes were as blue as the sky, the lines around them, deeper than Elizabeth remembered. "Have you missed me?" She hated to ask, but she needed to know.

Vivian said, "How've you been? Guess you learned to cook. Well, that's a useful thing to know."

A wave of disappointment washed over Elizabeth. She felt compelled to bring up the thing that she was sure loomed between them. "Look, Vivian. You know Jonathan wrote to me. That's to be expected."

"And you've wrote to him."

"A number of times."

"Did you tell him all about Montana?"

"Not all. Vivian, he's my fiancé. What am I supposed to do, ignore him?"

"No, Elizabeth. You're supposed to ignore me. You'll be gone pretty soon . . ."

"Not before July."

"That's soon."

"It's weeks and months away."

"It's tomorrow."

So Vivian had missed her!

Vivian ran her hand along her mount's neck. "I can't be thinking about your leaving, Elizabeth. We had a minute of time, a star in our hands, the moon at our feet. That's all we were allowed to have."

"But you sound like I won't see you anymore."

"You'll see me, but not like before. You belonged to somebody else before you ever got to Montana. Out here that's supposed to mean something."

Elizabeth clenched her hands into tight little fists at her sides. "Oh, Vivian, please . . ." She took Vivian by the hand and led her around the side of the house. "You can't do this. This is not what either of us wants, and we both know it. Right now there is you and me and all of this lovely country to share together."

"You hated it four weeks ago. Polly told me how you behaved in front of Marcus Donavan."

"She had no right to talk about it. I was afraid."

"Maybe you'll always be afraid."

"But I move forward, don't I?"

"Not without complaining."

"I've been brought up a little differently than you, Vivian. I haven't been expected to do *anything* other than to look beautiful."

"You look that, all right."

"That wasn't my point."

"Could have been."

They had drifted behind the house now. The windows were on the other side. They were alone. "You come here, Vivian Blake." Elizabeth snatched her and wrapped her arms around her. Vivian began to argue, to push Elizabeth away, but Elizabeth held firm. "You know what I'm going to do, Vivian, so let me have my way, and then I'll let you go home. If you don't, I'll scream."

"Then scream."

Elizabeth's lips came down hard on Vivian's, but she could have been kissing a fish. Vivian would not make a move, would not put her arms around Elizabeth, would not respond at all. Elizabeth stopped kissing her.

144

"Vivian, I love you. The love I feel for you could fill the space of Montana."

"It needs to fill the space of the world, Elizabeth. That's what's wrong with your love for me."

"And does yours?"

"Yes."

Her simple answer stunned Elizabeth, the shock of it rocking her from head to toe. But all she could think to answer was, "There is now, Vivian. This is what we have."

Vivian lowered her eyes, her face hidden beneath her hat brim. After a long pause, she spoke quietly. "And I'm a fool."

Vivian was giving Elizabeth something, some precious part of herself that was hard for her to relinquish. Tenderly, Elizabeth kissed her for it.

Vivian slipped her arms around Elizabeth and slowly pulled her close. She began to return Elizabeth's kisses, reluctantly at first, hard little pecks on the lips, one or two on Elizabeth's cheeks. But soon their kisses became an exchange between two longing lovers, lips fully meeting in a heavily charged moment.

Elizabeth wanted to lay Vivian down, convinced that the snow beneath them would turn to fragrant green grass and the golden sun would warm their bodies, that birds would sing and flowers would grow.

Vivian was the first to pull away. "I can't cope with this, Elizabeth." She held Elizabeth's face tightly between her gloved hands, and looked steadily into her eyes.

Elizabeth's heart lurched. Had Vivian changed her mind after all? Fearfully, Elizabeth waited for Vivian to tell her so, trying to prepare herself for the devastating words that would end her joy.

Vivian said, "You go on inside, gal," and Elizabeth's heart nearly stopped beating.

There was a look of intensity in Vivian's eyes. She spoke in a hoarse voice, "And don't you come out unless you're ready to learn how to be a sheepherder. We can scrub the stink off'n you before you go home. Your boyfriend need never know."

Elizabeth threw herself into the arms of the smaller woman, ecstatically happy. "Oh, Vivian," she uttered. She took a step backward. "I'll be ready in five minutes." She could barely contain herself. She wanted to run across the prairie and shout jubilantly to the earth and sky.

Vivian said, "You know it ain't going to be goose down you'll be sleeping on or eating rare beef steak cut up into little bitty pieces. It'll be musty Montana feather and tough mutton. You go get ready now if you think that's what you want."

Elizabeth's head swam wildly. "Are you sure, Vivian?"

"If Montana is supposed to be half the heaven that folks is always claimin', then I guess this is the half they were talking about. We'll worry about the hell part, come July."

Chapter 12

"You may *not* go with her, Elizabeth! I won't let you." Polly stood before her niece, blocking her way to the door.

Elizabeth did not waver. "I've been invited, Aunt Polly, and I'm going." She had her light bag packed and had put on the pants that Vivian had pulled from a saddlebag and handed her just before she'd come inside.

Polly glared at her scornfully, her face a black cloud. "Look at you, wearing trousers! You don't look like any niece of mine."

"Stop worrying, Aunt Polly. I'll be fine. Give my love to Uncle Andy, and please tell him that I took Billy."

"Oh, no, you're not taking Billy," Polly rejoined sternly.

"Uncle Andy promised I could ride him while I'm here."

"Yes, here on *this* ranch."

Impatiently, Elizabeth stepped around her aunt. She felt trapped and was anxious to be outside and gone. "I'm riding to Vivian's camp, Aunt Polly."

Polly's eyes widened. "You're going to her winter camp?"

"The sheep are there. That's where Vivian needs to be."

Polly rolled her eyes and threw up her hands in consternation. "This is too much." She snatched a coat from the back of the door and flung it on as she stormed outside. In no-nonsense steps, she approached Vivian who waited quietly beside her horse. Elizabeth walked over and stood resolutely by Vivian's side. "See here, Vivian Blake," Polly said plainly. "My foolish niece tells me that you two are headed for your camp. You can go there if you want, but Elizabeth is staying here."

Vivian did not flinch before Polly's threatening stance. "We're going to my ranch first, Polly. We won't be starting for camp before tomorrow morning."

"My niece isn't going!"

"Elizabeth?" Vivian turned to her.

"I'm going."

"It's almost spring, Vivian," Polly pronounced, as though stating a national declaration. "A sheep camp is no place for Elizabeth. She's a lady. She's been brought up knowing no other life. It would be a terrible thing for her to see."

Quizzically, Elizabeth glanced from Polly to Vivian. She'd been to the camp. There was nothing much there. "What would be a terrible thing to see?" she asked.

Vivian waved away Polly's words as prattle.

Polly remained undaunted, determined to stop her niece. "Think about the weather. There may be a bad storm on the way. Or Billy might —"

Vivian put up a silencing hand. "I'll see she stays out of trouble and doesn't get hurt. Does that make you feel better?"

Polly leaned into Vivian's face. "Nothing will make me feel better unless Elizabeth stays right here." She repeatedly stabbed the air and pointed toward the earth. "My niece hasn't been here much at all since she arrived last July. Foolish independence! That's what it is. Just plain, foolish independence! And you've been no help at all, Vivian Blake."

Elizabeth put an arm around her aunt's rigid shoulders. "Aunt Polly, why did you and Uncle Andy leave the East and come to Montana?"

For too long, Polly pondered Elizabeth's question.

"Why, Aunt Polly?" Elizabeth insisted, already knowing the reason, a reason mentioned off and on over the years in letters Polly had written back home.

"To be free," Polly flashed back.

"And that is why I came . . . before I can no longer be free."

"It's not the same thing. *I* came here with your uncle. *You* are alone."

Elizabeth released her and moved closer to Vivian. "I'm not alone, Aunt Polly, and I'm not going to argue about it any longer. Besides, you're worrying me. You should be dressed warmer for this weather. You would tell me that, so please go inside before you catch your death of cold."

Vivian chuckled. "She sounds just like you, Polly."

Polly's eyes blazed with anger. "You hush your mouth, Vivian Blake." She turned to Elizabeth, her eyes softening. "I expect if you got sick, you could take care of yourself all right."

"I expect I could, Aunt Polly, thanks to you." Elizabeth gave her aunt a lavish hug.

At the door, Polly asked, "How long will you be gone this time?"

"I don't know," Elizabeth answered honestly. "I don't want to make any more promises that I can't keep." She looked toward Vivian. "I know I'll be just fine, though."

Polly shook her head. "Humph! Two days from now, you'll wish you were back here. Mark my words."

Elizabeth smiled. "Remember to give my love to Uncle Andy."

"As soon as he quits bellering at me for letting you go."

"You didn't let me go. I insisted." She embraced Polly one more time, determined that not even her aunt's disapproving eyes would make her change her mind.

"It's getting late, Elizabeth," Vivian said, as the women mounted up, "We'll have to make time. I want to be sure we get home safely."

"Don't worry so." She tried to seat herself more comfortably in the saddle, already feeling the unnatural pull of the stirrups against her legs and feet.

"I promised Polly."

Elizabeth knew that a word given by Vivian Blake, or, it seemed, by any Montanan, was a word kept. She must learn to do the same. "Of course. I was wrong to suggest otherwise."

The vast plains spread out before them, a clean blanket of snow broken only by occasional dips and animal tracks. The sky was a flat sheet of slate gray, encouraging the travelers to maintain a steady pace over the thick icy crust. Breath flowed rhythmically from the nostrils of women and horses; conversation and the crunch of hooves, accompanying the jingling harnesses and squeaking saddle leather, splintered the silence. From time to time a rabbit or a coyote came within their view, only to melt from sight almost as quickly as it had appeared.

Sometime later, the riders stopped before Vivian's barn door. There was an unusual stillness about the place. "Where are your chickens?" Elizabeth asked.

"Took them and the cow to camp last fall. They're a damn nuisance, but we all like eggs and milk."

Gallantly, Vivian helped Elizabeth to the ground. Elizabeth, ignoring her quickly stiffening joints, slid against Vivian's body and into her arms. Her lips were only inches from Vivian's. She wanted to press them against her own.

Vivian let her go and turned to loosen the cinch of her saddle. Her back to Elizabeth, she asked, "Did you bring your letters along?"

Frowning slightly, Elizabeth realized that she had been put off. She answered huffily, "I did."

Vivian pulled her saddle from her mount and draped it across a fence rail. "I thought you might."

"I have a right to read them."

"You love Jonathan, don't you?"

"Yes, I love him. We've discussed it enough. What do we have to do next?" Elizabeth wanted no more talk about Jonathan.

"We stable the horses and then we rest. There sure won't be any resting after we get to camp, I'm thinkin'."

"Will we ever be alone together?"

"Not after today. We'll be bunking in with the men. We'll use the bed. They've got a cot."

"So at least I'll be able to hold your hand at night."

" 'Bout all. Let's move. I'm cold."

An hour later, they sat before the hearth, their stockingless feet warming before a cozy fire, flickering flames casting dancing shadows across the room and its lazy visitors. Tantalizing odors filled the soddy as meat and vegetables simmered in a small cast iron pot hanging over the fire. Biscuits baked slowly in a Dutch oven at their feet.

"We'll have to be up and moving before dawn," Vivian said.

Does anyone ever do differently here, Elizabeth wondered irritably. She and Vivian hadn't yet kissed. Elizabeth knew it was Jonathan's letters separating them. That, and because she had said she loved him. She had felt so *guilty* saying it. And why should she have? Only this morning, she and Vivian had come to

152

an understanding. Vivian was not keeping her part of the bargain at all.

Vivian crossed her arms and wiggled her toes. "I noticed the sky's clearing off tonight. There could be a weather change coming. I'd just as soon take advantage of the crust while it's still thick enough to handle the horses' weight. It'd be harder than hell on them, busting through every five feet."

She fell quiet. Elizabeth reached out a foot to touch Vivian's, wanting to close the chasm between them. Vivian drew away. Elizabeth did not give up, moving closer to her, taking her hand and holding it tightly.

Vivian sat stiffly. "I think you better get the reading of your letters done."

"They can wait."

"That's not what you want, is it?"

If that was the game Vivian wanted to play . . . "No." There! Montana honesty.

"Get them, then."

Elizabeth went to her bag and extracted the letters. She could have torn them open in her thirst for word from Jonathan; however, in fairness to Vivian, she had been willing to wait for a time when she was alone to read them. But now she had committed herself, and feigning indifference, she sat on the bed and slipped a finger beneath the flap of an envelope.

Vivian looked her way. "You might as well bring them over here, Elizabeth. No sense in straining your eyes."

Elizabeth felt underhanded reading the letters in front of her, but it was Vivian's idea, after all, and she certainly could guess what they contained. Elizabeth thought she might as well not make them less than they were.

Jonathan had filled pages and pages with loving words. She read slowly, envisioning him, hearing his voice. He had never said aloud to her the things he had written down. It struck her as odd that he couldn't voice such romantic notions when he was with her. Vivian had, though: "A star in our hands, the moon at our feet" — words of a sensitive, loving poet. She blinked several times, realizing that her mind had drifted to another time, another world. She brought herself back from that world and read the rest of Jonathan's letters.

Slowly, she refolded the final page and then read the news from her parents. From their words, she could tell that they believed she had never strayed from Polly's side. She had told them many things about the Box R and the things she had done and learned there. She mentioned nothing outside the ranch.

She put away her mail and then returned to her chair. Vivian added big chunks of coal to the fire, cooling it down. She then dished up bowls of stew for them both. They ate quietly, Elizabeth uncomfortable from Vivian's long silence. She set her bowl aside. "Are the letters troubling you so much, Vivian?"

Vivian took a big breath and slowly let it out. "It ain't just them, Elizabeth." She rested an ankle across a knee. She often sat like that, and Elizabeth found it endearing. "I don't feel like there's just you and me in this soddy. I feel like Tom's here, too."

Elizabeth raised questioning eyebrows. All this time she thought that she alone was causing the tiff between them. "A ghost?" she suggested.

"Not a real one. But the only other person that's ever slept in that bed over there is Tom. I just keep thinking about that . . . and I feel a little strange."

"I want more than a dusty haystack for us, Vivian. I don't like to think that what occurred in Uncle Andy's barn is something that could happen between any stableboy and housemaid."

"I'm not suggesting we go to the barn. But I got my memories, just like you got your letters. As a matter of fact, look over there."

"What?"

"Your bag on the bed. Jonathan's letters are sitting in it, on top of old Tom's bed. Kind of curious, ain't it?"

Elizabeth smiled and nodded. "We both brought our ghosts with us."

Vivian grinned lopsidedly.

"It doesn't have to be like that. Vivian . . ." Elizabeth knelt before her and leaned against her knees, her hands resting lightly on Vivian's forearms. She could feel the heat from the fireplace warming her back. "It is very obvious to me that you still love your Tom."

"I miss him."

"We both miss our men. I think we're trying to decide how much of ourselves we're going to give to each other tonight." Elizabeth paused and smiled. "We've gotten into a very serious discussion, haven't we?"

Vivian chewed on her lower lip.

Elizabeth smiled again. "We're scared, Vivian. That's all."

"How come you know so much?"

"You know what I know."

"I'm going to take the pot off the fire now."

While Vivian banked the fire, Elizabeth removed her bag from the bed and drew back the covers.

Wordlessly, they undressed before the hearth, their backs to one another. From the corner of her eye, Elizabeth saw Vivian reach for her nightgown warming near the fire. "Don't," she said. "Don't put it on."

"But I always wear it."

"Not tonight." Elizabeth's ears roared with the sound of her bold words. She drew Vivian into the circle of her arms and closed her eyes. She stood flesh to flesh the length of Vivian — naked . . . naked . . . naked in her arms. How wonderful. How glorious!

Vivian's skin was cool, her body muscular. Elizabeth could feel small breasts pressing against her, with nipples as hard as pebbles. Soon she would take those nipples into her mouth. The thought of it made her head reel. But for now it was enough to feel the drumbeat of Vivian's heart against her chest, to feel her heavy breathing blowing across her shoulder.

She untied the ribbon from Vivian's hair, freeing it to fall across her back. Vivian loosened Elizabeth's, and, with their faces only inches apart, the taller woman's hair created an umbrella of seclusion around them.

An eternity passed while Elizabeth studied the flicker of light in Vivian's blue-violet eyes. Now and then a coal would snap and burst, illuminating their bodies for a fleeting second.

The heat warmed one side of them; their flesh cooled on the other. "Come," Vivian invited in a voice from deep within her throat.

They climbed between cold sheets, the tick rustling. Their teeth chattered as they tried to cuddle, their knees drawn to warm their own bellies.

"I think we'll do a whole lot better if we straighten out," Vivian said between clenched teeth.

They melted together, crushing themselves to one another, lips pressed, tongues exploring, legs entwined. They kissed a hundred times — or maybe it was only once.

They rolled one another over and over, thrashing about, the sheets and blankets forgotten, the heat from their bodies now enough to warm them.

They finally broke apart, Elizabeth's body over Vivian's. She nibbled at Vivian's lips, first the upper and then the lower and then slowly moved to her throat. This was as far as she had ever kissed Vivian. Now she would do what she had longed so much to do before. Positioning Vivian on her side, Elizabeth lay in her arms and took a breast in her mouth. With a soft sigh, she began to suck. She heard Vivian moan as she rolled onto her back; Elizabeth followed, her mouth still on her. Vivian expelled a deep breath, and her body shuddered.

Vivian ran her hand down Elizabeth's side, the tingling of her touch racing through Elizabeth like wildfire. In a throaty voice, Vivian whispered, "I love you, Elizabeth."

"I love you, too," Elizabeth managed to say. She found speaking almost impossible.

Vivian moved from beneath Elizabeth to her side, continuing to caress her from throat to thigh. Like gentle rain, Vivian's hair fell against Elizabeth's skin.

Elizabeth drew up her knees and waited for Vivian's touch. Vivian's lips found her throat and then each breast. Elizabeth was wild with longing for her as Vivian continued to kiss her, deliberately, sensuously, all the way down to her belly. Elizabeth dropped her legs, and Vivian rested her cheek against Elizabeth's hair and against her inner thigh. Elizabeth's mind was thick with passion.

Vivian moved up and pressed her mouth against Elizabeth's breast. She put a hand on her leg and with tortuous purpose she spread Elizabeth's soft folds and touched her. Elizabeth groaned loudly and bent her knees again, clutching Vivian to her.

Vivian moved her hand. The rhythmic motion brought Elizabeth to a burning climax. She spread her legs wide, her climax spiraling outward, totally claiming her existence. She throbbed inside, her own blazing flesh scorching her. She heard someone calling her name, telling her that she loved her.

Eventually, the sensations lessened until she was able to think again. She ached overwhelmingly, and she burst into uncontrollable tears.

Vivian moved to her side, cradling her in her arms, murmuring soothingly.

Elizabeth was filled with happiness. "I'm all right," she whispered. "I'm all right."

She held Vivian as she would hold a precious gift, kissing her over and over, covering her cheeks and eyelids and throat. Her hair fell forward, and with a handful she stroked Vivian's chest and belly.

She slipped her hand between Vivian's thighs and

then shyly, between her lips, and felt a softness in Vivian that sent tiny explosions of light through her mind.

Vivian opened her legs, allowing Elizabeth to freely touch her. Wondrous, Elizabeth explored Vivian's womanliness and all the heights and depths of her.

Vivian guided Elizabeth's hand into her, her body sucking on Elizabeth's fingers as she moved them in and out, touching soft, moist walls.

Vivian pushed Elizabeth's mouth to her breast, thrusting herself against Elizabeth. Elizabeth continued to press exploring fingers against her and in her, and she heard Vivian moan . . . plead, "Don't stop."

Elizabeth felt suddenly in control with a power she did not know one human being could have over another, although she had wanted the same from Vivian. "Oh, Vivian," she cried out. "How I love you. How I love you."

She felt the inner heat of Vivian, felt her hips rise as Elizabeth covered her with her body. Vivian gasped and raked her back with her fingernails, and then went limp, burying her face against Elizabeth. Lovingly, Elizabeth enfolded her in her arms.

Vivian clutched Elizabeth to her. "I'm going to miss you, Elizabeth. I already do."

Elizabeth's heart cracked. "Don't, my darling. We're not supposed to think of those things."

"I know, but I don't ever remember love being like this."

Elizabeth pressed her finger against Vivian's lips to stop her troubling words. "Never mention it again, Vivian," she said.

"Never," came a hoarse reply.

They turned to each other again, the sound of the crackling fire their only companion.

Chapter 13

Three packhorses in tow, Elizabeth and Vivian were headed for winter camp by five the next morning. Elizabeth repeatedly rubbed her tired eyes. She did not mind the exhaustion, and smiled until her cheeks ached every time she looked Vivian's way. Only the saddle beneath her disturbed an otherwise perfect day.

The women were bundled against the early morning chill, but by mid-morning they had shed their scarves and gloves. Overhead, a half-familiar sound attracted Elizabeth's attention. Hundreds of feet above flew several dozen flocks of geese. Soon, thousands of birds blanketed the sky, their honks filling the air.

"Chinooks coming," Vivian said as she watched the courtly V-formations float apart and then gracefully reform again. "We better step on it."

As the day lengthened the temperature rose, and the icy crust softened, the horses beginning to sink into its deteriorating surface. "We'll have to ride tonight, Elizabeth," Vivian told her. "We can't take the time to camp."

Elizabeth didn't complain. Sleeping on snow or riding a horse all night were both equally unpleasant.

That evening they stopped long enough to cook beans and bacon for supper and to grain the animals. In less than an hour, they were riding again. Elizabeth refused to think about her painful body.

They came upon a rapidly flowing stream. Vivian spoke with urgency. "We need to cross the gulches before noon tomorrow."

Elizabeth watched the small creek visibly swelling as it flowed by.

They rested for an hour around eleven before continuing steadily on, guided by the light of a bright moon. By late morning of the following day, the crust was gone, and the great drifts that had sculpted the land were cut in half. Simple brooks, bone-dry since early last summer, were near-rivers where the mountains' runoff had swelled them to dangerous proportions. Trees torn out by the water's powerful surge were snagged here and there along newly formed banks.

It was at the last of these streams that Elizabeth saw her first buffalo. Two lifeless bodies, badly

162

bloated, blank eyes staring from huge faces, legs and tails stiff, tumbled through the muddy waters. Elizabeth watched the shaggy carcasses roll by.

"Those old bulls must have been trapped in the hills all winter," Vivian commented. Silently, the women rode away.

They traveled ten miles downstream before finding a place to safely cross the rampant stream. On the opposite shore, they retraced the miles, reaching camp by one o'clock.

The odor and baaing of sheep were carried to them on chinook winds. A mile north of camp, the main herd grazed on a hillside. A second smaller flock was located nearer by to the south. A single mounted rider could be seen circling each herd.

As the women pulled up before the soddy, Vivian said, "You go inside and rest. I'm going to see Al and Henry first."

Gingerly lowering herself to the ground, Elizabeth replied, "You're as tired as I am, Vivian. At least have a cup of coffee before you go."

Vivian shifted in the saddle. "Can't take the time. You go on in."

Elizabeth turned to leave, expecting Vivian to ride away. But she, too, dismounted and followed Elizabeth inside. The door closed, and at once they moved within the circle of one another's arms, and kissed hard and passionately. Then Vivian stepped away. She stood with nervous uncertainty, fingering the brim of her hat. "I'm going to ask if you'll cook for us, Elizabeth. That's all you gotta do. But . . . I'm asking."

"I would spend the rest of my life cooking for you, Vivian, if I could." Elizabeth's words were out before she had thought. She had made a dreadful mistake.

Vivian opened the door. "For now will do."

"Of course." Elizabeth felt like a fool.

As she watched Vivian ride toward the herd, Elizabeth unloaded the packhorses and unsaddled her own, turning them into a nearby corral already holding Mike and Skip, the team used to draw the sheep wagon. The pair trotted over and nickered greetings to the new horses.

Here at the base of the mountains, grass was plentiful, protected throughout the winter by the steep eastern slopes. The horses craned their necks beneath the bottom railing, nipping off the buffalo grass between their big teeth and noisily grinding it to a frothy pulp.

In the soddy's doorway, Elizabeth wistfully looked toward the bed, wishing she could collapse upon it and sleep. Instead, she put on a plain dress, no longer able to bear men's pants, and got busy building a fire in the stove and storing things away. She made coffee, and when it was ready she drank three cups, piping hot and black as coal, while she cleaned the room.

It was evident that the men had had no time to care for the place. She washed and put away dishes and picked up clothes carelessly tossed about. She stripped the bed in which the men had been sleeping. Tonight she would set up the cot stored beneath it, for whichever of them came. There would be little room, but they were all going to have to manage. Fortunately, with the weather rapidly changing, Henry and Al were sure to move into the wagon soon.

She remade the bed with the fresh sheets and blankets that she had insisted Vivian bring along. She was glad that she had, because the covers now destined for the cot smelled strongly of sheep. She would give the bedding a good airing, but she expected it would be of little help.

Taking along a bucket, she sought out the cow and set about milking her. It was harder than milking a goat, and she hated the cow as much as she had hated the goat. In a henhouse located out back of the soddy, she searched beneath the squawking, protesting chickens, finding only five eggs.

Parked next to the soddy was a small, low-built wagon that looked to be a henhouse on wheels. A single row of four small compartments were built side-by-side, each with its own little door. Elizabeth checked for eggs there, too, but found none.

Uncertain of when the herders would be in or how many at a time, she had to have hot food ready and plenty of it. She set bread to rise, and prepared johnny cake, potatoes and meat. She carried out her duties thinking little about them. Only back home would it make sense to boast of the speed with which she had lighted the coal or mixed the bread or speedily baked rolls.

She ate johnny cake and molasses, saving the eggs for the others and then stepped outside, looking toward the northern herd. The distance didn't seem so far off. She had once imagined a mile to be inaccessible on foot. In Montana it was a step away. Tired as she was, she decided to walk over and see Vivian. Everything was ready at the soddy. All she had to do was pop the bread into the Dutch oven and feed folks whenever they came in.

Taking along the coffee pot and a couple of cups, she started out. She found the exercise loosened her stiff joints and sore muscles, making her feel much better.

Twenty-five minutes later, Vivian and Al rode over to her and dismounted, fully appreciating her efforts.

"Glad to see you, Elizabeth," Al said. He took his hat off to her and smiled, warming her heart. She thought he meant it, and not just because of the coffee.

He drained his cup quickly and with visible concern said, "We better get moving, Vivian. Thanks a lot, Elizabeth. Good coffee." He mounted up, nodding to her as he rode away.

"Why is the herd divided up?" Elizabeth asked.

"Come on," Vivian said. "I was just headed over to Henry. I'll take you back and tell you on the way."

"Only if I can sit sidesaddle," Elizabeth insisted.

Vivian grinned as she helped Elizabeth and then handed her the pot and cups before climbing up behind her. "The other herd is the drop band. They're pregnant ewes, and none of us is going to have a minute's peace until every one of them is done birthing."

"I see." Elizabeth felt her cheeks burn. She must come to grips with ranchers' straightforwardness.

Vivian tightly held Elizabeth around the waist all the way to the house. She slid off the horse's rump and helped her from the saddle. "It seems like I keep telling you I have to go."

"I'll see you later," Elizabeth answered. She smiled and waited for Vivian to ride away before going inside.

An hour later, Henry came in, a blanketed bundle carried carefully in his arms. "Howdy, Missy. Saw you ride in with Vivian. We sure can use you. Here, I brought you a bummer. Her momma's dead, and I can't get any of the ewes to foster her. They'll be more bummers coming, but I wanted you to have this first one for your own."

Elizabeth sat down with the bundle and gently pulled back the blanket, revealing a miniature black face, its bright eyes squinting in the light. In awe, she whispered, "Oh, Henry, she's beautiful."

"You won't think so when she starts getting into everything, and you're tripping over her all the time."

"Why are you doing this?"

"Vivian speaks highly of you."

"Vivian speaks too much."

"Wouldn't know."

Elizabeth looked again at the yeanling. "What do I feed it?"

"Milk, water, and molasses. We got bottles over there." Henry handed her one. "Mix the vittles equal. She'll take it. She'll be thinking you're her momma, Missy, I gotta warn you."

Softly, Elizabeth touched the lamb's head. "That'll be quite all right, Henry." She could not possibly have given up the tiny creature. Keeping it well wrapped, she put it on the floor before the stove. "Let me get you a plate, Henry."

"I'll do it myself, Missy. You need to feed that there baby. And keep feeding her. Let her stand when she eats, and hold that bottle up so's she thinks she's feeding from her momma. Keep her plenty warm, too."

Henry ate quickly, and was gone before Elizabeth had finished feeding the bummer. "I'll just call you Bummer, little lamb," she said. "They'll laugh at me, I'm sure, but I don't care. Do you know you're the first pet I've ever had?" Lovingly, she stroked the kid as it sucked and jerked at the nipple, milk slobbering out of the sides of its mouth; its tiny blatts sounded like sweet music to her ears.

Off in the distance, she could hear the occasional barking of dogs and the continuous blatting of sheep. She had just lit the lanterns and sat down to relax for a minute when Vivian came through the door.

Elizabeth rose to greet her, glad that she had finally decided to stop and rest. She couldn't wait to show her Bummer. "Look what Henry brought —"

Vivian waved her off. "Don't have time, Elizabeth. Could you get me something to eat? I have to go right back out."

"So soon?" Elizabeth fought rising disappointment. She had so wanted to show off Bummer and to spend some time with Vivian this evening.

"The ewes are dropping lambs all over the place. We can barely keep up with them. And they ain't going to stop just because night's coming." Vivian sank into a chair and took off her hat, tossing it on the table. She rested her head in her hands.

Quickly, Elizabeth set food and coffee before her. "Who's with the drop band?"

Vivian dug into her meal. "Both Henry and Al."

"But what about the other flock?"

"We're praying the dogs do their part," Vivian answered, grabbing another roll.

Elizabeth sat down across from her. "It seems as though you're awfully shorthanded."

"Just terrible. We need two people at the drop band and one with the dry herd. I had two extra hands last year. Man and his wife. She cooked. He herded. They moved to Texas last summer. Said they were going into cattle. Sheeping was too damn much work."

The exhaustion in Vivian's voice was plain. Elizabeth thought her own job as cook was going to be easy next to what Vivian and the men had ahead of them.

Vivian pushed back her empty plate. "I got another man coming, but he ain't due till next week."

"What about me? I could help."

"You are helping. You're cooking."

Excitement flared in Elizabeth's chest. She could become a true working member of this outfit. "I could drive between the flocks and cook from the wagon. You and the men could sleep in shifts inside until your extra hand gets here."

Through the winter, the sheep had worked their way along the mountains' lower eastern slopes, steadily moving toward the soddy. Now the animals would drift out onto the prairie as the snows receded. She could return daily to camp, taking care of chores and replacing depleted staples and supplies. The men and Vivian need not come back at all.

Vivian looked thoughtful. "Be a big job . . . but it would get us fed faster. And usually we do just sleep on the ground, but the wagon would be nice now and then."

"Are you coming in tonight? Any of you?"

"It don't look it. You and me got here just in time. I thought we had at least another three, four days before those babies were due. Damn sheep. Can't ever tell what they're going to do next."

"Eat," Elizabeth ordered, dishing Vivian a second helping. As Vivian turned back to her plate, Elizabeth began to gather supplies together.

Vivian gulped her supper and then gave Elizabeth a quick hug and a kiss on the cheek. "Good food, Elizabeth. Wonderful. Don't forget the dogs when you're packing grub." She left in darkness, carrying a lantern with her.

Grinning widely, Elizabeth puffed up with pride. She was glad Vivian was not there to witness it.

She harnessed Mike and Skip by lantern light. She was in no mood for pranks, and a painful twist of an ear or a sound pinch on the nose immediately brought each gelding into line. After much grunting and sweating in the cold night air, she hitched the team to the wagon. She put out a hand and rested against Skip's flank. She was shaking and rivulets of sweat ran down her face. Only then did she realize how nervous she had been about handling these two horses again. She stood aggressively before the big beasts and looked menacingly at them. Pointing a shaking finger into their faces, she warned, "Well, you sons of guns. I'm boss now. You hear? Don't you ever mess with me again."

An unexpected loud snort in her face made her jump. Disgusted, she glared at them both.

She scurried around to load the hot food and everything else she thought she would need to feed the crew and dogs for the next two days. She tucked

Bummer snugly into a box near the wagon's tiny stove already warm with a low fire. Hanging lanterns on either side of the wagon to light her way, she drove toward the drop band.

She found Henry on the near side, kneeling before a dead lamb. Lantern light gleamed off the shaft of a long knife held in his hand. Blood stained the ground around him, and beside him, a newborn stood on wobbly legs.

Jumping from the wagon for a closer look, she arrived just in time to watch the herder slice the dead animal from tail to throat. Expertly, he peeled the hide from the carcass and shook it right-side-out. He grabbed the yeanling and drew the hide over its head as it bleated loudly in protest.

Elizabeth stared wide-eyed at the lifeless body, stripped and so carelessly discarded to one side, its existence no longer important. "Shouldn't we at least . . . eat it?"

"Nope. Born dead and no telling why. Ain't got enough meat on it anyhow. Cook it up for the dogs if you want."

Elizabeth left the dead animal untouched.

Henry picked up the cloaked lamb and walked toward a lone ewe mournfully blatting into the night. He approached the animal slowly, speaking softly. "Here's your baby come back to you, momma." He offered the lamb to the ewe and then set it on the ground beside her. The sheep swung her head around, cautiously sniffing the strange baby. She nudged it once or twice, nearly knocking it off its feet. The lamb bleated and butted the ewe who watched it as it searched for her udder. As it found a teat, the mother continued nosing its body.

171

"Good," Henry said. "Looks like she'll take him."

Elizabeth quietly came up behind him. "Was that her own baby back there?"

"Yep. That's whose coat that there little bummer is wearin' now. Only he ain't gonna turn out to be no bummer. We fooled momma with her own baby's pelt."

Elizabeth hustled back to the wagon, happy the orphaned yeanling was going to have a mother but happier still to have something to occupy her mind other than thinking about the skinned lamb. She brought Henry a cup of coffee. "Sugar or milk?"

"Neither," Henry answered. With a bloody hand, he reached for the cup.

Elizabeth blinked rapidly and looked away. "Where is everybody?"

"Vivian's with the other herd right now. Al's over there. See his light?" He glanced at the wagon. "Did you bring your bummer?"

"Of course. She's going to be the best ewe you've ever seen," she pronounced.

A tiny smile played at the corners of his mouth. "You're gonna spoil her, Missy. She won't know if she's sheep or human."

Elizabeth laughed and took Henry's cup, avoiding looking at or touching his hand.

She drove to where Al was busily assisting a ewe. Mesmerized, she watched from her seat. She had never seen anything being born before. She wasn't even sure how it all happened. The amount of blood staggered her. How on earth could the animal survive? There was a gush of fluid as a large, slimy-looking sack was quickly expelled from the animal's rear. Al broke the sack with a small knife

172

and drew from its watery contents a soggy lamb. He swabbed its nose and put his fingers in the lamb's mouth, clearing it of some unrecognizable substance. The mother rested for a few minutes, then stood and began to wash her baby. Hand to her mouth, Elizabeth jumped from the wagon and walked hastily to the back. She leaned heavily against the tailgate, taking several deep breaths to bring her nausea under control.

Shortly thereafter, Al came over. He put a fatherly arm across her shoulders. "You all right, Elizabeth?"

"I'm fine," she lied. "I —"

"It ain't no place for a lady."

"It's no place for anyone!"

"You get used to it."

"I've brought food . . ." She gagged as the birth flashed in her mind.

"I'll help myself," Al said.

With a handkerchief, Elizabeth wiped sweat from her brow. "Don't tell the others, Al, please. I'll get better."

He put his arm around her shoulders. "I know you will, Elizabeth. You're real game. How about some coffee?"

Gratefully, she took the cup he offered.

He gave her an encouraging pat on the back, thanked her for supper, then turned back to the herd. Held high above his head, his lantern cast long, swaying shadows across woolly backs as he slowly threaded his way among the flock, searching for ewes and lambs in need.

Elizabeth slid a hand beneath Bummer's blanket, touching the sleeping animal. She closed her eyes and whispered, "Oh, lordy, am I in trouble, Bummer. Your momma has a lot of toughening up to do in this sheep business."

Chapter 14

Even after Jolly Hughes, Vivian's extra hand, arrived at winter camp, everyone was still badly overworked and short-tempered. It was a difficult time, as lambing continued without letup for a month. While the crew labored day and night fighting for every yeanling's life, Elizabeth kept busy driving between the two flocks and the soddy, cooking for the crew and taking care of all the animals.

She learned that the henhouse on wheels was not a henhouse at all, but a lambing wagon. Vivian had had her use the team to move the wagon over to the drop band and park it there. Somehow, it had become Elizabeth's responsibility to look after any ewe refusing to care for her young. Through brute force, she would push and prod the reluctant mother up a small ramp and into a compartment, and then quickly throw her lamb in behind her. There, the ewe would remain for hours, or days if necessary, until she willingly allowed her baby to nurse. The sheep could be very swift, and four times out of five a ewe escaped before Elizabeth was able to shut the door. Grinding her teeth, she would mutter with exasperation each time she had to recapture the wayward animal.

Along with the duties of the lambing wagon, she now had twelve bummers in her care, tiny little things that needed to be fed constantly and at all hours of the day and night. The bummers slept in boxes in the sheep wagon. And when she parked, the older lambs easily got around, following her every step, making demands on her, blatting, and running in play.

Tired as she always was, seldom sleeping more than five hours at a stretch, Elizabeth showed no signs of fatigue until one morning when she ran pell-mell across the prairie after the bummers, screaming at the top of her lungs, and threatening them with a frying pan. She had mistakenly rested on the ground while cracking six precious eggs into the griddle. Without warning, the babies had bounded across her lap, flipping the pan upside down. For the first time in her life, Elizabeth had flown into an uncontrollable rage. Gasping and crying, she finally came to a stop beside the wagon, her pan hanging dejectedly at her side and watched as the tired lambs curled up together in a ball beneath the vehicle. Never again would she sit on the ground to prepare food.

Elizabeth was convinced that the ever-dirty, heavily bearded Jolly Hughes was purposefully making her feel uncomfortable, talking more than a man should, laughing uproariously over nothing, and saying lurid things about the ewes. At least he always slept near the herds, never using the wagon's cots as the others occasionally did. But working in shifts made it likely she'd be alone when he came to the wagon to eat.

One day she complained to Vivian about his ill-bred behavior. Irritably, Vivian cut her off mid-sentence. "We need him," she said sharply. "You're going to have to bear it for a while, or just tell him to shut up."

Elizabeth was devastated that Vivian would not stand up to Hughes in her behalf. Jonathan would have beaten him to a pulp.

The following afternoon, Elizabeth again found herself alone with him.

"Howdy, little lady."

Normally, Elizabeth would have smiled weakly at him, handed him his plate of food and moved to the other side of the wagon where Hughes would talk around great gobs of food, muffled words designed to embarrass and humiliate her cast her way. She could allow it no longer. Sarcastically, she answered, "Howdy, little man," and shoved his dish into his stomach. Her heart thudded in her chest.

Hughes froze, his eyes locking on hers. "I ain't no little man, *little* lady." He knocked the dish aside and grabbed her, towering over her.

177

"Perhaps you're not even a man," she said contemptuously. "Especially a gentleman." Ignoring the fear and anger in her breast and the pain in her arm, she looked unflinchingly at him.

"Bah!" Hughes exclaimed, and released her.

Elizabeth picked up his plate and refilled it, handing it to him, ready to do battle again if need be. But Hughes ate the rest of his meal silently and quickly and afterward stalked off toward the herd.

Thereafter, he bothered her less, and if he did, she was ready for him.

The long month of March came to an end, the final lamb was delivered, and much to Elizabeth's great relief, Jolly Hughes departed. Weary sheepherders now wandered over to the wagon in pairs to sit and chat and, at last, joke pleasantly among themselves. The last traces of flatland snow disappeared under unusually warm skies and winds. Early grass had rapidly sprung up, bringing back birds and animals and biting insects that Elizabeth constantly swatted away.

Vivian and Henry were sitting with Elizabeth on boxes, leisurely eating supper and sipping coffee as the bummers wandered between their feet.

"We're going to work on the lambs for a few days," Vivian told Elizabeth, "and then bring the whole flock back to the ranch."

Elizabeth poured herself a cup of coffee. "What's left to do?"

Henry looked at Vivian to explain. Vaguely, she answered, "Oh, not a whole lot."

"Then what's left?" Elizabeth asked again. She picked up Bummer, who settled in her lap like a well-trained dog.

Henry lowered his eyes, and Vivian cleared her throat a couple of times.

"Come on, you two," Elizabeth said. "I've been through enough around here. You don't have to treat me like a china doll."

Henry took off his hat and scratched his forehead. "Missy," he began, "we're gonna render the boy lambs incapable of bein' fathers."

Elizabeth shuddered inwardly. The terrible pain the tiny animals would have to endure.

"It'll be good when this difficult time is over," she said flatly.

"Well, that ain't quite all there is to be done, Missy," he said.

"Not all?"

Vivian rubbed the back of her neck. "We need to dock their tails and notch their ears."

Elizabeth eyes widened as she looked at her bummers romping nearby. "More cutting? Isn't castration enough?"

Vivian pursed her lips, and Henry studied his plate. "We'll be needing to do your bummer, too," he told her.

"But she's mine," Elizabeth protested. "I don't want you hurting her, maiming her." She hugged Bummer to her chest. The lamb wriggled from her grasp and jumped to the ground.

"She needs to be docked and branded, Elizabeth," Vivian declared firmly. "She's a sheep first, a pet second."

Tenderly, Henry said, "Out here, Missy, there

179

ain't never any real pets. Everybody has to work. Your lamb will have to join the herd and be a momma someday."

Elizabeth started to argue, but Henry kept on. "Here, an animal works just like a person, Missy. Nobody's excused. That's the way of it."

Elizabeth stood and walked off by herself. They were always saying something like, "That's the way of it," or "It can't be helped," or some such philosophical trash. They had no hearts. She couldn't even have one tiny thing but that it had to have some greater purpose than just plain being loved.

She turned and faced them. "I thought Bummer was my pet. All mine."

"She ain't never been all yours, Missy. Nothin' is ever all anybody's. That's the way of —"

"I understand, Henry." Just as she understood that Vivian was not all hers, and she could never be all Vivian's. Henry's point was driven home unmercifully.

He stood, saying uncomfortably, "I better be gettin' back." He walked off leaving the women alone.

Vivian rose and put her plate on the back of the wagon. "I'm sorry life's so hard for you, Elizabeth. I'm really sorry."

"Everything is such a surprise to me," Elizabeth replied. "Nothing is ever simple. I don't know if anything will ever be simple again." She stared absently at the horizon. "I just don't know."

"Come here, love." Vivian led her to the other side of the wagon, away from the men. She held Elizabeth's hands, caressing the backs of them with her thumbs. "I miss you," she said.

Elizabeth looked at her. She was small, yet strong in many ways. Her words did not fit that strength. "I miss you, too, Vivian. I want to hold you. I want you to hold me, to make everything all right."

"I can't fix the pains of the world, Elizabeth. Sometimes I can't even fix my own."

Elizabeth knew she referred to their coming separation.

At the end of five days, the lamb docking, castrations and earmarkings were complete. Elizabeth had watched none of it, and when Bummer and the rest of the little lambs had been brought back to her, she had privately cried over their misfortune. She had bathed their ears, but the bummers would not let her touch their tails.

The spirits of the entire outfit ran high. They had been on the trail four days now. There had been no problems to slow them down. The torrential streams had receded, making traveling less hazardous, and tomorrow they would all be home.

Bummer rode on the seat beside Elizabeth, the remaining lambs and the chickens in the lambing wagon drawn behind the sheep wagon, and behind that, attached to a stout rope, came the cow. Renewed prairie grass, bent softly beneath the team's hooves and the wagon wheels, filled Elizabeth's nostrils with the sweet scent of spring.

She arrived at the final night's campsite well ahead of the rest, the shepherds traveling at the pace of the lambs. She turned her own lambs loose and then expertly freed and hobbled the team. She looked in all directions, broad plains of green buffalo grass, yellow, red, and orange flowers just beginning to blossom, and endless blue sky spread out before her. Her eyes filled with tears. How could she have even for a moment felt dwarfed by Montana? How lucky she was to have had a chance to be here, to experience this space, to fill her mind with wonderful memories. She would miss it all terribly.

She would miss Vivian.

Impulsively, she threw herself face down onto the prairie floor, tightly clutching the grass between her fingers, the blades' rough edges harmless against her calloused hands. A shorter blade tickled her nose, and she sneezed with a jerk and then buried her face again. She rolled over several times before coming to a stop on her stomach. Insects buzzed about her, and she compared their sounds to the sounds of symphony orchestras she had heard in the city. The insects won.

The lambs came over to her and butted at her sides and head, trying to get her to play. Two stood on her back. She did not try to shake them off.

She longed to lay Vivian down on the vast sea of grass and rest naked on top of her, the warm winds stroking their bodies. She pretended that Vivian was beneath her, the hard ground acting as Vivian's muscular body, the soft grass the more tender part of her. Elizabeth breathed harder as she thought of their long night together before they had come to winter camp. Her thighs ached, her breasts ached, her lips burned. She wanted to beat her hips against the earth.

She fell asleep, and when she awoke she lay unmoving for a long time, then rose and checked the sun. She had learned that when it was three feet above the mountains it was time to start the fire.

When the evening meal was near completion she fed the lambs. As soon as they reached Sheephaven the bummers would join the herd. As much trouble as they had been, she would miss them. She hoped her lamb would not have to go right away, too.

In half an hour she heard the distant sounds of the flock. She looked in its direction, spotting a rider coming her way.

Like a whirlwind Vivian came galloping across the prairie, flicking her reins from side to side, driving her horse at top speed. She came to a thundering stop, flinging herself from the saddle, running the last few steps to Elizabeth. Even with her tiny frame she nearly swept Elizabeth off her feet. Their lips came together, a blaze of heat coursing through Elizabeth's body. They broke apart, looked intensely at one another and then kissed again, tightly clutching each other. At length they parted, breathless, tense, wanting more.

"I came on ahead," Vivian said.

Elizabeth laughed loudly. "Oh, Vivian, I love you so."

"I love you, too, Elizabeth. I love you too."

They looked toward the west, the sounds of the flock growing stronger. "They'll be here soon," Elizabeth said.

"We can hold each other for a few minutes on the other side of the wagon."

They hurried behind the vehicle and the second they were concealed, they were again in each other's arms, their lips smearing one another's faces.

Between kisses, Vivian uttered, "We'll be home tomorrow."

Elizabeth ran her hand along the side of Vivian's cheek. "Will we be alone?"

"Only at night. Shearing is going to begin, and that'll —"

"Shhh." Elizabeth put a finger against Vivian's lips. "We can talk about that later."

The next few moments were precious jewels of time with nothing else existing in their world. Elizabeth pressed her body hard against Vivian; her breathing became heavy, the want of Vivian overflowing her mind. "Oh, God, Vivian, I can't stand how much I love you."

Vivian kissed Elizabeth, searching her mouth with her tongue, pressing her hands against Elizabeth's breasts. She gasped aloud and slipped her arms around Elizabeth's neck. The sounds of sheep, men, and dogs told them they must part. "One more night, Elizabeth."

"And then I will hold you and never let you go."

Vivian's voice became hard, her eyes penetrating. "If only you meant that."

Elizabeth blinked in confusion. She rubbed a hand across her forehead, feeling the heat of her skin. "I didn't mean to sound possessive."

Reluctantly, Vivian released her. "You know I want you. To hell with Jonathan."

Why, Elizabeth questioned, did they both keep talking about . . . things? They had agreed not to. Was it deliberate? On Vivian's part, yes, but what about herself? Desperately, she looked at the nearing herd. There was no more time left to discuss all this. She kissed Vivian quickly and then let her go.

Together they watched the herd approach. The dogs began to bunch the sheep while the men slowly circled the flock, halting its forward movement.

Vivian rejoined the men, and Elizabeth busied herself with supper. This day was almost over and the crew would be coming in to eat. In spite of the unresolved conflict between Vivian and herself, Elizabeth could barely wait to go to bed so that when she awoke in the morning she would be able to say, "This afternoon we'll be home, and tonight Vivian will sleep by my side."

She would think about nothing else.

Chapter 15

Since returning to Sheephaven late in the afternoon, Elizabeth was as busy as ever. She wanted to be sure that things were somewhat taken care of in the house so that in the evening she could devote all her time to Vivian when she returned from working with the flock. There would be all day tomorrow to tend to other details.

Elizabeth had left the wagons parked before the house, and after releasing the chickens she stabled the team and milked the bawling cow before turning her out to pasture. The motherless lambs had been taken to the herd, but Bummer was still with her, following her everywhere and frequently getting underfoot.

Elizabeth lighted several lanterns, and rushed in and out of the house unburdening the sheep wagon of its boxes, bags, barrels, cooking gear, and staples, setting everything down helter-skelter throughout the kitchen and parlor.

In the bedroom she tore the mattress tick off the bed, emptying it outside, quickly restuffing it with new grass until the tick looked grotesquely fat. She remade the bed, bouncing on it several times to flatten it a bit before she could tuck in the sheets. Twice, Bummer jumped up beside her, and twice Elizabeth took a shoe to her.

From the small clothes bag she had taken to winter camp Elizabeth laid out fresh underwear and a clean dress.

She dragged in the bathtub, setting it before the hearth, and started a big fire. She filled the tub with water heated on the stove and then locked the kitchen door. After quickly bathing and dressing, she emptied the tub and heated more water for Vivian. She fed Bummer, and the lamb curled up beneath the table and fell asleep. Elizabeth was more than glad her pesky little friend had finally settled down.

She baked biscuits and made a stew the men could eat in the bunkhouse. She had no sooner removed the biscuits from the oven when Vivian and Al arrived. She kept enough food for herself and Vivian and sent Al off with the rest.

Scanning the kitchen, Vivian declared, "Good Lord, Elizabeth, what a mess."

Elizabeth smiled, taking Vivian's hat and coat.

"Tomorrow," she said, tossing the wraps aside. Hungrily, she took Vivian in her arms.

They kissed, Elizabeth hardly daring to believe that for the rest of the night Vivian was hers.

Vivian leaned her head against Elizabeth's shoulder and closed her eyes. "God, I'm tired."

"I've set up the tub. I'll scrub your back. You'll feel better."

Vivian tightened her arms around Elizabeth's neck. "What a wonderful idea."

Elizabeth was vastly pleased with herself.

She lowered her head, her mouth meeting Vivian's in a tender, lingering kiss. Vivian's lips parted to accept her exploring tongue. Breathless, they parted.

"I think we should eat," Elizabeth whispered against Vivian's forehead.

After supper, Elizabeth prepared Vivian's tub. She went to fetch cold water while Vivian undressed. When she returned, Vivian stood nude facing the fire. Elizabeth paused to look at her, the smooth lines of her back tapering down to her graceful hips and bottom and strong legs. "You are utterly beautiful," she said.

Shyly, Vivian covered her breasts with crossed arms. "I'm freezing," she answered. "But thank you."

Elizabeth poured the cooler water into the tub and checked the temperature.

Vivian climbed in. With a soft moan her eyes closed, she leaned her head against her knees. Elizabeth began to wash her back. "I've never had such care," Vivian said dreamily. "You could spoil me with very little trouble."

Vivian sat up, letting Elizabeth wash the rest of her body, both women smiling, their cheeks flushed, giggles breaking forth. But Elizabeth hurried. She was thinking of other things, and she knew that Vivian was, too.

Wet and gleaming, Vivian stepped out of the tub, and Elizabeth briskly rubbed her warm and dry. "Come on, get into bed," she said.

Clutching the towel around her, Vivian weaved her way through the clutter and into the bedroom. Elizabeth threw back the covers, and Vivian climbed in.

It took Elizabeth only a moment to undress and join her. They snuggled together, the tick pleasantly rustling beneath them, its fresh odor pleasing.

"New feathers," Vivian remarked. "You have been busy."

"I'm going to pretend I'm lying out on the prairie," Elizabeth said. "And that's as much make-believe as I'll need. All the rest will be real."

She turned out the lantern beside the bed, and they lay in each other's arms for several minutes, luxuriating in unaccustomed comfort.

"I can't believe I'm in a bed," Vivian said. "It seems like it's been centuries."

Elizabeth laughed quietly. "It was."

She slid a leg across Vivian and then straddled her body, fitting herself against Vivian. Vivian's fingers traced an erratic pattern across Elizabeth's back. Cold chills raced up and down her spine.

Elizabeth smoothed back Vivian's hair. "I've dreamed about this moment for a long time."

"It wasn't easy sleeping in that wagon with you just across from me, and not be able to touch you," Vivian whispered.

"I know." Elizabeth's lips brushed lightly against

189

Vivian's as she deliberately tormented herself, prolonging the kiss that would start this night, delaying the physical gifts they would share. Deliberately, she trailed a path along Vivian's upper lip with her tongue.

"Oh, Elizabeth," Vivian whispered. "I want this night to last forever." She pressed her mouth, hard and demanding, against Elizabeth.

Their lips locked as Elizabeth moved to Vivian's side. With feather lightness, she drew her fingers across Vivian's body, circling her nipples, breasts, and the soft lower parts of her belly. Vivian quivered beneath her touch.

Her breathing heavy, Vivian opened her thighs. Elizabeth pushed aside the blankets and slowly slid down, resting her head on Vivian's belly.

Vivian arched her back as Elizabeth's cheek brushed against damp hair. She smelled Vivian's womanly scent, and she eagerly pressed her lips against her.

Vivian locked her fingers in Elizabeth's hair, holding her captive, her words unintelligible. She bent her knees wide, and Elizabeth thrust her tongue deep within, searching beckoning depths and shallows.

Her mouth came to rest, tongue pressing firmly on swollen flesh, then rhythmically thrust against the hardened place.

Vivian's body became rigid, hands clutching Elizabeth's shoulders. She cried out "I love you. Elizabeth, I love you."

She went limp, and Elizabeth released her, wiping her face against the sheet. She moved to Vivian's side. "You are completely enchanting."

Through the window, pale moonlight cast its glow across Vivian's face. She smiled and softly kissed Elizabeth, then moved to Elizabeth's breasts to take a nipple in her mouth. Elizabeth quietly moaned, ripples of desire streaking through her.

Elizabeth lay back, and Vivian moved over her, placing herself between Elizabeth's thighs. Elizabeth raised her legs, wrapping them around Vivian.

With tender nips, Vivian pulled at Elizabeth's breasts. She moved a hand to Elizabeth's thighs, resting a flat palm against her hair. Gently, she slipped a finger inside, pressing against Elizabeth's wetness.

Elizabeth's hips lifted rhythmically, tremors washing over her, gaining speed. Hungry intensity swallowed her and she cried out once, twice, and then drifted away on wave after wave of ecstasy. She collapsed, spent, unable even to speak, cradled in Vivian's arms.

They lay quietly beneath the blankets, their breathing steadying as time slid by. In the background, the fire cracked and flared. A coyote howled in the distance.

Elizabeth rose and moved over Vivian.

Elizabeth was glad that Vivian had gone off with the men the next morning. They would dig a trough for dipping sheep, Vivian had told her. Had Vivian stayed, Elizabeth was positive that nothing would get done by either one of them.

Lost in thought, Elizabeth closed her eyes. "Ah,

well," she said, returning to the present. She needed to finish baking bread and peeling potatoes, and she hadn't yet emptied a single box.

Even with the door open, the heat of the stove on this warm day made her feel as though she were standing up to her neck in hot water; sweat coursed down her body. She wore her hair piled on her head, strands hanging down, tickling her face. Her skirt was hitched high, the sleeves of her blouse pushed back, the front unbuttoned to her bosom. She was barefoot, the floor boards cool against the bottoms of her feet.

Bummer wandered in and out, and Elizabeth smiled at the animal as it collapsed beneath the table.

She moved the bread into tins and rubbed an aching foot against her leg. Impatiently, she brushed hair out of her eyes, leaving a smear of flour across her forehead. Her nose itched. Scratching it, she left a second streak across the tip.

Without warning, Bummer tore out from beneath the table in a playful mood and slammed painfully into her shins. "Damn it, Bummer," she yelled. "Watch where you're going!"

"Elizabeth?"

A shadow filled the doorway. The bright light behind the man blinded her, but she recognized his voice instantly. "Jonathan!"

Bummer ran outside, brushing against his pants. Jonathan shied away from the lamb and then stared open-mouthed at Elizabeth.

She fumbled to button her blouse and gave her skirt a yank. Why, she wondered wildly, was he here, not just in Montana — but here — at Sheephaven?

"Elizabeth," he repeated. He tossed aside his hat

192

and stepped around boxes to reach her, crushing her to him, kissing her deeply. He stepped back, holding her at arm's length. In a deep voice, he stated, "My God, it's good to see you."

She looked up into his dark eyes. "I . . . You're here. How did you find me?" Her hands shook as she tried to straighten her hair, leaving behind traces of flour. And her shoes! They'd been kicked aside somewhere. She looked so terrible she couldn't even be glad he was here.

He towered above her, his big frame filling the room. His hair and beard were as black as coal, and tiny crow's-feet at the corners of his eyes deepened with his smile. His nose was narrow and his lips full over strong white teeth. He had come dressed for calling in a dark business suit, hat, and tie, looking remarkably comfortable on such a hot day.

"Your Aunt Polly wrote me. She sounded very worried."

Critically, he studied her, and again she brushed at her hair. "I'm . . . fine," she answered. "I'm happy . . . you're here." She glanced past him. Had Vivian seen him yet? They had to talk!

Jonathan cast a reproving look around the kitchen. "This isn't exactly where I expected to find you."

His obvious displeasure in the place jarred her. "We just got back from camp yesterday," she explained. "I haven't had a chance to put things away."

"Why are you here at all? Your letters said you were staying with your aunt and uncle."

"I have been —"

"But not much," he interrupted.

Elizabeth tried to laugh. "Not as much as Aunt Polly would like, I admit, but —"

"You have flour on your nose," he said softly, gently brushing it off. "I missed you, Elizabeth. I worried about you."

He held her close to his chest, and she rested against him. He felt so *big* next to Vivian.

"I've come to take you back to the Box R," he said. "I would like you to leave right now."

"That's impossible. I have to put things away. And I'm the cook. I have to —"

"Don't be silly, darling." He fussed at wayward strands of hair around her eyes. "You don't have to do anything. You're not one of them. Let them do their own cleaning and cooking. What in the world are you doing working at all?"

"Vivian asked me if I would help, and I agreed. I can't just walk out on her."

"But, my dear, I've come two thousand miles to see you." His voice was firm, authoritative, his smile fixed.

Nervously, she answered, "I understand, Jonathan, but I gave my word."

"Such high-minded principles from my little girl." He smiled easily, finally releasing her. He sat at the table, and she offered him coffee, still shaken by his startling presence.

"How was your journey?" she asked.

He leaned back in the chair and unconsciously pinched the bridge of his nose between thumb and forefinger, a habit, Elizabeth had learned, he occasionally displayed whenever he was overly tired or angry. She guessed he was probably both right now.

He had come such a long way for her — and she didn't present a very lovely picture.

"There are still some terrific drifts in the mountain passes," he said. "At one point, in some God-forsaken place in Dakota Territory, we were badly delayed because of several big drifts. Perhaps they were snowslides. The engineer went through them by backing up the train a mile and then opening the throttle full blast. He would ram the snow, making a dent two or three car-lengths long, then he would back up another mile and do it all over again until we reached the opposite side. I don't know how many drifts we overcame that way. People were jarred unmercifully by the jolts and terrified out of their wits. Why, Elizabeth," he said fretfully, "two or three times a day for a week, every man and boy had to help dig out the train. I told the engineer that traveling first class I wasn't going to lift a shovel. He had the gall to tell me no one was traveling anywhere unless everyone worked. So I did, because I knew it meant I would reach you sooner. But I can tell you I plan to write a letter to the Northern Pacific tomorrow. It took me four weeks to reach Billings on that miserable trip — food rations . . . water rations. And then there was the coach ride to the ranch and the long drive from your uncle's. I'm glad to stop moving, if only for a minute." He ended his tirade, looking terribly weary.

"Oh, Jonathan," she said sympathetically, only' now beginning to recover from his sudden appearance. "I'm so glad you're here." She sank into a chair beside him, placing her hand on his sleeve. She wanted to tell him of all the new things she had learned, the wonderful people she had met. She wanted him to meet Vivian.

He smiled at her, looking boyishly happy. "Change your clothes, darling. We'll leave right away."

"I'll just finish up my tasks," she said. "I need to be sure that rascal of mine will be all right, too."

His eyes registered surprise. "That lamb is your pet? I thought you hated animals."

"Why would you think that?" She opened a box and quickly put things away.

"I've never known you to have a pet or to even mention one."

"I haven't, but I've always wanted one."

"Well then, we can get you a little kitten when you get home."

Somehow she found the idea of a kitten not very appealing. "They can't do much."

"That's the idea," he said. "You wouldn't have to do anything except to open the door for it once in a while."

"I'd like to see an animal be a little more active than that." Bummer would romp and run and butt up against Elizabeth and blatt her brains out whenever she was hungry. Bummer was full of life.

As if on cue, the lamb strolled inside and began begging for food. "It's time to feed her," Elizabeth said. Bummer followed her from spot to spot as she prepared a bottle, and when it was ready, rapidly emptied its contents. Elizabeth continued unpacking, and Bummer settled beneath the table.

Jonathan raised his eyebrows. "Aren't you going to throw it out?"

Mildly surprised, she asked, "What for?"

"A sheep in a house," he said disgustedly. "I hope you aren't planning to take it back to New York."

She started to explain that Bummer would certainly remain behind, but before she could he asked in an accusatory tone, "Where are your lovely clothes? And good Lord, Elizabeth, you're not even wearing shoes."

"It's hot, Jonathan. I'm alone here . . ."

He left his chair and took her in his arms. "Oh, Elizabeth, Elizabeth, my darling. I don't mean to scold, but I never expected to find you living under these sordid conditions. And your mouth. That terrible scar. What, in God's name, has happened to you while you've been away?" He raised his hand to touch the mark.

Irritated by his gesture, she turned her face away. "I tripped and fell against a rock during a hail storm." She deliberately ignored his second question.

"*A hail storm?* What were you doing out in a hail storm?" The muscles beneath his beard jumped spasmodically. "I want you to leave this place — now!"

She pulled away from him and braced her hands against the back of a chair, gripping it until her knuckles turned white. "You should have waited for me in New York, Jonathan," she said with as much patience as she could gather. "Then you wouldn't have been disappointed in what you see. I'd still be the same fine lady you knew before I came to Montana. And," she added angrily, jutting out her chin, "stop yelling at me!"

He lowered his voice, but still he growled at her. "Frankly, you look like a scullery maid. How can you

197

stand this pig sty? And the stench of this entire farm is unbearable!"

She glared at him, disappointed that he could think so little of Sheephaven before even having seen it. She retorted, "You get used to it."

Jonathan picked up his hat, his entire posture one of determination. "Get your things together. We're going."

Be damned, she thought. He wouldn't dictate to *her*. "Stand aside, please. You are in my way." She grabbed two buckets and headed out the door.

Jonathan trailed after her, waiting while she pumped water. Impatiently, he took the heavy buckets from her as she started back to the house.

For the next two hours, he followed her around the ranch while she milked the cow, gathered eggs, and swept out the bunkhouse. In the house again, she put everything in order and finished preparing that evening's meal. She had planned to do other things and to rest from time to time as the day's weather demanded of any rational person, but Jonathan's obvious displeasure as he tagged along beside her drove her on.

She finished by making the bed she and Vivian would have shared tonight, the thought tugging hard at her as she fluffed the pillows and threw the quilt across the sheets.

She wiped a perspiring brow with her forearm and looked around. For such a small place, it required the work of two people to properly keep it up. Elizabeth wondered how Vivian would manage now. "The same way she did before you came along," she whispered.

In the parlor, Jonathan sat impatiently waiting, his hat dangling from his fingers. "All ready?"

"I must leave a message for Mrs. Blake," Elizabeth said, "and then we can leave."

She left the note on the table and went into the bedroom to quickly pack her bag.

"I saw him. He's quite a man."

Elizabeth jumped. She hadn't heard Vivian come in.

"Mr. Stanton is waiting outside for you. I've already tied Billy to the buggy."

"Thank you." Elizabeth stopped what she was doing and looked steadily into Vivian's eyes. "I didn't expect him, Vivian. I had no idea."

"Polly?"

"Yes."

"Well . . ."

"Come, I'll introduce you."

"No need. I talked to him. He's a fine man, Elizabeth. I can see he has great concern for you. No doubt he loves you very much."

Elizabeth put the last of her things in the bag and strapped it shut. "Supper's on the stove whenever you and the men are ready. Chores are done. The house is back to normal."

"Thank you."

Elizabeth briefly hugged Vivian, not daring to linger, hardly daring to look into her eyes. Vivian, too, was brisk and business-like as she linked her arm through Elizabeth's. Together, they walked out to the buggy.

"Here she is, Mr. Stanton. No worse for wear."

"Some," Jonathan answered.

Elizabeth watched him reach for the bridge of his nose.

"Well, I'll admit . . . some," Vivian conceded.

"But not much. She's strong, your promised. She'll be a good working wife."

"My wife won't work, Mrs. Blake. She won't have to."

"Well, she's a lucky one, I'm thinkin'."

"Come on, Elizabeth." He assisted her into the buggy.

Speaking very carefully, Elizabeth said to Vivian, "Thanks so much for having me." She hoped her eyes betrayed nothing.

Vivian tipped back her hat. "Sheephaven thanks you for all you've done, Elizabeth Reynolds." She propped a boot on a wheel spoke, directing her words to Jonathan. "This week they'll set up spits for a pork and beef barbecue roast. The shearing crew's due any day. Be about fifty of them. Why don't you and Miss Reynolds come over when things get moving? I'll send word."

Jonathan replied, "I don't think Elizabeth —"

Enthusiastically, Elizabeth grabbed Jonathan's arm. "Let's come, Jonathan. It'll be wonderful to see."

Vivian had told her of the bold men who rode from sheep ranch to sheep ranch all the way from Mexico to Canada, wearing colorful clothing and riding on beautifully hand-tooled, silver-trimmed saddles and outstanding horses. They were a wild group, laughing and carefree. But when they changed into their work clothes and took up the shears, the wool piled up rapidly, most men shearing over a hundred sheep a day.

"I don't think it's appropriate, Elizabeth," Jonathan said, possessively taking her hand in his.

"Better not miss it, folks," Vivian encouraged. She

continued to lean comfortably on the wheel. "It'll be your only chance. Gonna be shearing contests, too. There'll be big money bets, if you like to gamble."

"Jonathan," Elizabeth pleaded.

"We'll see, Mrs. Blake," he answered briskly. "Meanwhile, it's getting late. We must be going."

"Sure." Vivian dropped her foot and backed away from the buggy.

"Goodbye, Mrs. Blake," Elizabeth said. Her heart ached unmercifully. She was not prepared to leave Sheephaven — to leave Vivian.

"Goodbye, Miss Reynolds, Mr. Stanton." Vivian took off her hat, shading her eyes with her hand.

Jonathan nodded politely and began the drive toward the Box R, Billy trailing behind.

Elizabeth glanced back to see Vivian waving. Elizabeth returned the wave, maintaining heavily guarded control over her tumultuous emotions. She looked back once more, but Vivian was no longer in sight. Elizabeth closed her eyes, fighting to clear her mind of Vivian Blake, and linked her arm through Jonathan's.

They rode silently for some time. The sun began to kiss the horizon. Falling shadows played among the grass and sage as a cool breeze rippled through the land. Low to the ground, a red fox streaked across the prairie.

"God, that woman is crude!" Jonathan burst out.

"Jonathan! What a cruel thing to say." Anger flooded Elizabeth's breast, and she withdrew her arm from his. "Mrs. Blake is a friend of mine and I'll not have you speak of her that way." She gathered that he must have been dwelling upon Vivian since meeting her.

" 'Ain't.' 'I'm thinkin'.' I don't see how you can possibly consider someone who doesn't even speak decent English a friend."

"Oh, don't be trite," she retorted. "What difference does it make how she speaks?"

"She offends my ears — and my eyes. A woman working on a sheep ranch, dressing like a man, acting like a man. Did you see the way she propped her foot on the wheel?"

"She's trying to carry on since her husband's death. I find her very noble."

"She should sell out and get married."

"For goodness sakes, Jonathan, she's not the only woman around here who runs a ranch."

Firmly he declared, "We're not going to that pig thing she's proposing."

"It's a sheep-shearing contest. The pig thing is what everyone will be eating." Pettishly, she couldn't help adding, "Along with the beef."

"We won't be going."

After weeks of being away, Elizabeth walked into the Box R ranch house. While Andy took care of the rig and horses, Polly fussed over Elizabeth and Jonathan. "I'm so glad you're both here," she pronounced happily, taking Jonathan's hat and coat and Elizabeth's bag. "I'm just so glad."

"I'm glad, too, Aunt Polly," Elizabeth said, as Polly repeatedly hugged her.

When Andy returned, they gathered in the parlor. They ate cookies, drank lemonade, and continuously interrupted each other, everyone anxious to talk.

Jonathan laughed and said, "I was afraid I was going to have to drag Elizabeth out by the hair on her head, Polly. She was determined to put things straight before she left."

Elizabeth felt her pleasant reunion with them begin to crumble. Jonathan needn't have put her leaving Sheephaven in such a contrary light.

"And did you put things straight?" Polly asked her.

"Not quite the way I wanted to," Elizabeth answered. "But I came close."

"If you did your best, Elizabeth," Polly answered, "then I'm proud of you. Anyway, you're here now, where you belong, and that makes me happy."

Pursing his lips, Jonathan nodded his assent.

Andy asked, "Will you be going right back to New York, Jonathan, or are you going to stay for the sheep shearing?"

"We'll be going home. I can't stay away from the factory too long."

Elizabeth eyed him coldly. "Who is we, Jonathan? You're not including me, I hope."

"Of course I am, Elizabeth," he answered impatiently. "What do you think I came out here for? Polly's letters said . . ."

Elizabeth glanced sharply at her aunt. "I'm trying to forgive you for that, Aunt Polly. Tattling!"

Polly reddened, her hands fluttering bird-like in her lap. "He needed to know, Elizabeth. Why, you were turning into an unfinished woman. You're too fine to be working."

Elizabeth stood abruptly. "I'm tired," she said. "I'd like to lie down. Is my room still the same one?"

"Of course, dear," Polly answered. "I put the

window up for you a little while ago. It'll be just right in there."

Elizabeth curtly thanked her and then faced Jonathan. "I'm not leaving here before July, Jonathan, so please don't include me in your plans." Annoyed with them all, she left.

Jonathan followed her. At her door, he asked, "May I come in?"

She hesitated, then stepped aside.

Resting his hands lightly on her waist, he looked perplexed as he studied her eyes. "I don't know you anymore, Elizabeth."

"You assume too much," she said. She leaned against his chest, trying to ignore the ill-humor gripping her.

His voice softened. "Let's not argue, darling. We've done nothing but fight today."

Well, *she* hadn't started it. "Then say nothing about my leaving Montana right now."

"Agreed."

He kissed her, his beard and moustache reminding her of Bummer's woolly hide.

And then she remembered — she had never even said goodbye to her little lamb.

Chapter 16

Life was easy now that Elizabeth was back at the Box R. She had only to crook a finger and Jonathan was at her side opening doors, assisting her with her chair, helping her into and out of the buggy, handing her a parasol, taking her arm as they strolled together. He made her feel cared for and womanly. After several days of it, she began to feel slightly irritated and then helpless.

And they didn't talk. At least not the way she had expected. She had imagined telling him all about her adventures. She had tried, once mentioning the mice at Vivian's soddy, and another time, the snake beneath the backhouse. Both stories, meant to be funny, had only angered him. He chastised her for going off alone. She told no more stories.

Jonathan planned to leave in two days. He had said nothing more about her coming, too. She loved him. She had told him so several times, but she would be glad when he was gone.

She cried at night, missing Vivian more than she imagined she ever could. She wondered how Vivian was and what she was doing. She assumed that shearing was going on now and that all of Sheephaven would be terribly busy. She considered driving over to see the shearers at work after Jonathan left, though she'd promised him she wouldn't. But what would be the harm if she never got out of the buggy?

Besides, she wanted to see Vivian.

The sounds of desperate pounding on the front door jarred her awake. She could hear Andy yelling, "I'm coming, I'm coming," followed by Polly's high-pitched voice. "It's trouble. I just know it's trouble."

Elizabeth got up and looked out the window. Light was just beginning to streak the horizon. The unexpected sight of Henry's horse created a stab of fear in her throat.

Polly shouted, "Elizabeth, you come out here right away!"

Elizabeth's hands trembled as she threw on a dressing gown and rushed into the kitchen, ardently praying under her breath, "Please, God, don't let anything be wrong with Vivian."

Jonathan came in from the parlor, his bed the couch since his arrival.

Nervously, Polly wrung her hands. "Vivian's asking for you, Elizabeth."

"Bad trouble, ma'am," Henry replied. He ran the brim of his hat around and around in his shaking hands. His obvious unrest suggested only the worst for Vivian.

"What's the problem?" Jonathan asked.

Quickly, Elizabeth introduced the two men. Henry said, "Vivian's real bad sick, Missy. It's her side again. She's been out of her head all night. She's been calling for you even out cold. I'm on my way to Billings to get the Doc."

"She pulled out of it last time," Elizabeth suggested hopefully. Terror continued to build steadily within her.

Henry shook his head. "Not this time, Missy. I stayed with her all day yesterday, and Al stayed last night. She wasn't no better when I left a while ago."

"I'll go to her at once." Elizabeth turned to leave.

Jonathan put out a hand, stopping her. "I don't think you should, Elizabeth. You don't know what to do."

She looked at him contemptuously. "I know what not to do, Jonathan. And that is nothing. Now, let go of me."

Polly patted her shoulder. "I'll fix you some food to take along."

Satisfied that Elizabeth was on her way, Henry started for the door.

"Get a fresh horse from the corral," Andy told

him. He pulled on his boots, saying to Elizabeth, "I'll saddle Billy. The buggy will be too slow."

"Hurry, Elizabeth," Polly encouraged as she gathered things together. "Change your clothes. You can wear a pair of Andy's pants. Jonathan, you go along with her."

Elizabeth squeezed Polly's arm and glanced at Jonathan. His face was white and rigid with anger, his fingers irritatingly rubbing the bridge of his nose. God, how she was beginning to hate that trait in him.

She left to dress, overhearing Jonathan ask Polly, "Does she know how to ride?"

By the time Elizabeth and Jonathan were ready, Andy had the horses saddled and waiting out front. Polly had already stuffed the saddlebags with rations. Rapidly, she advised Elizabeth. "Sounds like Vivian's got inflammation of the bowels. You keep hot salt packs on her stomach all the while she feels sick. I gave you plenty of salt and there's two quarts of good whiskey in there. Get her to drink it. It'll kill some of the pain. Make her eat, too. Gruel would go down easiest. Remember, whiskey and gruel." Quickly, she embraced Elizabeth and Jonathan.

As Elizabeth put a foot in a stirrup, Jonathan placed his hand on her elbow to assist her. "Damn it, Jonathan," she snapped. "Quit wasting time and saddle up."

Looking hurt, he moved to his horse.

Polly grabbed Elizabeth's hand. "I have to warn you, Elizabeth. Vivian isn't likely to make it."

Angrily, Elizabeth pulled away. "She'll *make* it, Aunt Polly."

Elizabeth and Jonathan loped at a steady pace. An experienced horseman, Jonathan rode well. They traveled cautiously in the rising heat, stopping at water found in draws, alternately walking and trotting the horses, reaching Sheephaven by mid-morning.

Ignoring her pain and stiffness, Elizabeth was first to dismount. She hurried inside while Jonathan grabbed the saddlebags.

Al sat by Vivian's side. "Glad to see you," he said, and acknowledged Elizabeth's quick introduction of Jonathan.

Vivian was awake, her eyes shiny with fever as Elizabeth knelt beside the bed. Slowly, Vivian turned her head. "Elizabeth," she whispered weakly.

Tenderly, Elizabeth wiped Vivian's damp brow. "Shhh, I'm here now. You're going to be fine." Seeing Vivian this way nearly ripped the heart out of her chest.

Vivian closed her eyes, and Elizabeth hastily spoke to the men. "I need water, Al, and bring a cot in here. Jonathan, get a sheet out of the dresser. Rip it into small pieces."

She went into the kitchen, lifted the stove lid and threw in several cats. She piled on cow chips from a box beside the stove and with a flick of her thumbnail, lighted a match. In seconds she had a roaring blaze going.

Jonathan came in from the bedroom and stood watching her, his eyes widening as he recognized the dung in her hands, saw the careless way in which she dusted her palms against her pants, the practiced ease with which she lighted the match against her shapely nail instead of striking it against the stove. He came over and placed a hand on her shoulder. A disturbing shadow crossed his face. "I wouldn't like to think this life is something you enjoy."

But it is, she thought.

Firmly, he reminded her, "You're going back to the Box R tomorrow."

"Of course," she agreed. She wouldn't be leaving tomorrow. Vivian was going to need her help for several days to come.

Al brought in the water, and Elizabeth emptied the salt and water into a big iron skillet, swirling the salt around until it dissolved. She said, "Jonathan will be staying in the bunkhouse, Al."

Already on his way out the door, the big man said over his shoulder, "Follow me."

Jonathan had no choice but to go, the planes of his cheeks quivering as he clamped his mouth shut and hastened after his retreating host.

Elizabeth returned to the bedroom. She drew back the covers and lifted Vivian's gown. She wondered who had helped her into it. It didn't matter. Someone had been kind to her. It saddened Elizabeth deeply that she had not been the one.

Vivian's right side was badly swollen, the skin taut and pinkish. She held it and moaned deeply.

Elizabeth lowered the gown. "I'll have a hot pack on you in a minute, Vivian dear." She jumped up and poured a stiff jigger of whiskey. Supporting Vivian's head, she held the glass to her pale lips. "Try to drink a little," she encouraged. "Aunt Polly said it would help."

Vivian sipped and coughed, grabbing her right side again.

"More," Elizabeth gently insisted.

Vivian drank and coughed again, but less forcefully this time. She lay quietly and then spoke in yet a weaker voice, "Glad you're here."

Elizabeth swallowed hard and fought off overwhelming alarm for Vivian's life. "Rest now," she told her.

Vivian closed her eyes.

The salt water was boiling, and Elizabeth threw in several pieces of cloth. She fished out one and then gingerly folded the steaming rag into a pad, carrying it in to Vivian.

Vivian rolled toward her. Barely able to make herself heard, she uttered, "I love you, Elizabeth." Already her body looked wasted, her eyes sunken, her skin sallow.

Elizabeth softly kissed her burning cheek. She placed the pack on her gown. Vivian covered Elizabeth's hand with her own, watching her through fluttering eyelids.

Later, Elizabeth prepared gruel and fed her a few spoonfuls. Vivian vomited, and Elizabeth wiped her clean and changed her gown. In an hour she fed her again, and once more Vivian threw up, but this time Elizabeth had placed a towel beneath her chin, sparing her the agony of being redressed a second time.

Late that night, an exhausted and grizzled-looking Doctor Evans arrived. He inspected Vivian, palpating her side, asking questions that Vivian could barely answer. She scarcely moved anymore, and had stopped eating altogether.

In the kitchen Evans said to Elizabeth, "You can just make Mrs. Blake comfortable, ma'am. I'm afraid she's got inflammation of the bowels."

"What does that mean, exactly?" Elizabeth remembered Polly's fatal diagnosis.

"Here, ma'am," Evans said, avoiding her eyes. "These pills will help some. That's all I can do. I'll see Mrs. Blake in the morning before I leave." He picked up his bag and hat from the table. "I know my way to the bunkhouse."

Alone in the kitchen, Elizabeth was gripped with sickening dread, its talons slipping around her mind, squeezing out her ability to think or to even move. She shook herself free of the terror, hating herself for weakening. She closed her eyes, breathing deeply until she was in control again.

"I'll take care of you, Vivian dear," she vowed. "*I* will pull you through. And *damn* all the unbelievers." She did not hesitate to add a prayer or two.

Throughout the night she applied hot packs to Vivian's side and encouraged her to drink sips of whiskey and eat bits of gruel. As she wiped Vivian's face and arms with a cool damp cloth, Elizabeth fought back ever-threatening tears.

The next morning, Al and Henry stopped by. Wordlessly they stood beside Vivian, sadly shaking their heads. Elizabeth refused to look at their discouraging faces.

Doctor Evans had long since come and gone, leaving more medicine and little hope. A short time after Al and Henry left, Jonathan came in. Vivian was sleeping, and Elizabeth felt it safe to leave her for a minute. She steered Jonathan into the kitchen.

He immediately took her into his arms. "Al said he'd take over here so you could go."

Incredulous, she stared at him. "Don't be foolish, Jonathan."

"You agreed you would go with me this morning."

"I cannot. Vivian needs a woman's hand."

"I can't believe you're the only one available. Polly could help out."

His voice had begun to rise, and she shushed him. "That's true. But I'm the one Vivian asked for."

"Oh for God's sake, Elizabeth." He flung up his hands and moved away. "You wouldn't walk into a place like this in New York."

"My friends don't live in places like this in New York."

Again he came to her and held her, his brow deeply furrowed, his eyes reflecting bewilderment. "I don't know you anymore, Elizabeth."

"Please understand, Jonathan." She looked steadily at him, trying desperately to make him see. "You know that I love you, and my being here was just supposed to be a wonderful vacation before we married. But somehow the vacation turned out to be a pilgrimage into real life. It's not the game I thought it would be." She took his face between her hands. "When Vivian is well, I will come home. I won't wait until July as I had planned. But I'll be here several more days at least. Will that satisfy you?" Even to think of leaving sooner caused her stomach to knot up, and she wondered why she was giving in.

His whole face lit up, and he gave her a solid squeeze. "That would suit me fine." Enthusiastically he said, "I'm going to Billings, Elizabeth. I'll wire the factory telling them I'm extending my time. But only until this is over, you understand."

She understood.

He added, "Apparently this is something you have to do. When you're finished I'll get my little girl back. I'm tired of fighting it and I'm tired of feeling bad about it. I'll return here in a few days. Get some sleep while I'm gone. You look terrible."

They kissed and parted, and again Elizabeth was at Vivian's bedside.

For the next week Vivian lay deathly sick; her body grew increasingly thin. Polly drove out a couple of times, bringing food and dresses, one of which Elizabeth gladly changed into. Polly stayed overnight both times, supervising Elizabeth's doctoring and relieving her so that she could sleep. Other women from surrounding ranches visited as well, bringing covered dishes and fretting over Vivian.

At the end of the second week another cot was moved into the parlor for Gerdy Truman, Bill Truman's wife, from Owl's Creek Ranch. Gerdy was a plump, good-natured woman with a weathered face and laughing eyes, and every bit as efficient as Elizabeth. Thereafter she and Elizabeth took care of Vivian together.

Despite Gerdy's steady help and cheery voice Elizabeth still slept fitfully, ate little, and constantly worried over Vivian.

"Child," Gerdy scolded one day. "You don't have

to be hovering over Vivian Blake every blessed minute. Now go on with your Mr. Stanton and take a walk. I don't want to see you till this afternoon."

Chastised, Elizabeth put on a sunbonnet and wandered off with Jonathan, who had returned several days ago. They walked over to the vats where the flock was being dipped, the shearers having left days ago. There were several unfamiliar men and dogs and a large flock of milling sheep and somewhere among the throng was Bummer. Elizabeth looked for her, realizing how much she missed her little lamb. She quickly gave up hope of finding her without Henry's help.

The shorn animals looked thin and naked without their heavy wool coats, and everywhere loud blatts filled the air. In single file the sheep were herded through a long narrow shoot. Dug into the earth, the shoot was filled with a dark, horrible-smelling liquid. The more stubborn sheep were booted in, but every animal had to swim for dear life, their hooves barely touching bottom.

Unexpectedly, a sheep leaped into the vat. Elizabeth and Jonathan jumped back, both narrowly escaping being splashed. Elizabeth screwed up her face against the stinking odor, exclaiming to one of the men, "What *is* that horrid stuff?"

A stream of tobacco juice landed three yards from the herder's dusty boots. "Sulfur, tobacco, herbs, and medication, ma'am. Kills ticks, treats cuts, an' makes wool grow better." The man stuck out a pole and unceremoniously rammed the head of a sheep beneath the dip. The animal emerged wild-eyed, swimming and bleating in terror to the end of the trough. It scrambled up a cleated ramp only to be greeted by a waiting dog who herded it toward a second flock, there to be branded.

Jonathan took her elbow. "You've seen enough, Elizabeth."

Impatiently she answered, "Another minute, Jonathan," and walked toward the branders.

Beside a man was a bucket of green paint. With a wide brush, he expertly swabbed a large S on the rump of a sheep. A second man grabbed any sheep not yet marked, and with a sharp knife deftly notched its ear.

Elizabeth turned away. She didn't want to see the sheep cut. She couldn't stand seeing any animal hurt.

"Come, Elizabeth," Jonathan insisted, and this time she followed him without argument.

A mere thirty minutes had passed since she had left the house and yet the sun made it too uncomfortable to remain outdoors.

"We could go to the bunkhouse," Jonathan suggested.

Inside, the cottonwood building was as cool as the house. There was an open window at each end of the small structure and bunks enough for six men. Next to a pot-bellied stove in the middle of the room sat a table and four chairs. Elizabeth took a seat and wiped her brow with a lace handkerchief.

Jonathan sat opposite her, concern evident in his worried gaze. "You look tired, darling. Would you like to lie down?"

"No, thank you," she replied, lowering her eyes.

"It'll be all right," he answered. "I'll sit by your side. We can talk. You can sleep if you like."

216

He was so kind to her. Since he had returned, he had spoken only pleasantly to her. He had worked, too, drawing water, cleaning stalls, and once even turning a hand at baking biscuits under Gerdy's strict guidance.

Elizabeth lay down on his bunk, and he drew a chair alongside. He sad down and took her hand. Tenderly, he leaned over and kissed her.

They chatted comfortably for a while, and eventually she fell asleep, thinking that when she returned to New York she would be happy.

A couple of hours later they walked arm-in-arm to the house. As she and Jonathan entered the door, Gerdy grabbed her hand. "Elizabeth, you need to come with me right away. You'll have to excuse us, Mr. Stanton. Woman's work to be done."

Gerdy's clipped words filled Elizabeth with renewed dread. Had Vivian grown worse while she had been gone?

Gerdy dragged her into the bedroom. "Look," she exclaimed. She drew back the covers and lifted Vivian's gown.

Elizabeth's heart beat wildly as she studied Vivian's side. She didn't dare believe her eyes. "The swelling's going down," she whispered.

Smiling widely, Vivian placed Elizabeth's hand against her naked belly. "Feel," Vivian said in a voice stronger than any Elizabeth had heard her use in weeks. Her skin was cool and her stomach less taut.

Elizabeth's eyes overflowed with tears. "You're getting better, Vivian."

"It doesn't hurt so much." Vivian pulled down her gown.

Gerdy beamed. "You're gonna make it, Vivian."

"Always knew I would. Had reason to." The thin woman looked directly at Elizabeth.

"Well, you gave us all a good scare," Gerdy told her sternly. "Knew a man once. Went through the same thing you did. He didn't make it. Knew another who did. He never took sick again."

Elizabeth held Vivian's hand. "And you won't either, Vivian. Do you want something to eat?"

"Not gruel," Vivian said.

"No, not gruel," Elizabeth promised. "Not stew either. You may have the broth, though."

Elizabeth supported her while she ate, and Vivian kept down the broth and drank some whiskey. "Just to keep you calm," Elizabeth said.

Vivian closed her eyes and fell into a peaceful sleep.

Gerdy left to find Henry and Al, anxious to be the one to deliver the good news. Elizabeth stayed by Vivian's side, watching her steady breathing, studying the gaunt face, now and then straightening Vivian's gown or the sheet covering her.

Three days later Vivian said, "Tomorrow, I'd like to sit outdoors for a while. You'll still be here won't you?" She looked anxiously at Elizabeth.

"I'll be here for as long as you need me," Elizabeth promised.

"How's Mr. Stanton?"

"He's fine."

"You'll be going home soon, I expect."

"Yes."

"You ought to know, Elizabeth, that I'll never love anybody the way I love you."

"Vivian . . ."

"Let me have my say, Elizabeth. I already know how things are and are gonna stay."

It wasn't fair of Vivian to speak of things in her heart. It would only cause them both pain.

"You behaved just like a well run dry when you drove off with your beau, Elizabeth," Vivian said. She grasped Elizabeth's hand, clutching it with surprising strength. "I don't know how you did that. I couldn't. I came in here and bawled my eyes out. Haven't done that since Tom died."

Her words pierced Elizabeth's heart — just as Elizabeth knew they would.

"Didn't you cry just a little?" Vivian asked.

"Of course I did, Vivian dear."

With great satisfaction Vivian said, "I knew you loved me. You always acted it."

"It was never an act, Vivian."

"How do you feel now?"

"You should rest, my darling." Elizabeth could not let her continue.

She started to move away, but Vivian clung to her hand. "I need to know," she insisted. She closed her eyes and lay still for so long that Elizabeth thought she had fallen asleep, but she opened her eyes again. "How do you feel?" she asked again.

"The same."

"Damn Eastern answer. Give me something a Montanan can understand."

Elizabeth kissed Vivian's hand, and took a deep breath. "I will open my heart just this one time for you Vivian. Then we must talk of it no more."

Vivian breathed deeply, appearing to relax.

"I love you. I will always love you . . ." Elizabeth began.

219

"As much as you love Jonathan?"

"Yes, but . . . differently."

"I don't understand how you can love two people at the same time."

"I don't either, but I do."

Vivian let out a long sigh. "Well, at least I can get on with my life knowing somebody once loved the hell out of me."

Elizabeth smiled painfully. She leaned close to Vivian's ear with words for her alone. She felt that she was losing control of the situation. "I . . . I would love to have gone mad with you, just once, out on the prairie somewhere, away from men and animals."

Their cheeks touched, softly resting against each other.

"Under the stars," Vivian whispered.

"And moon."

"We should have, that time we went to winter camp alone."

"We weren't ready."

Elizabeth felt her heart begin to pound in her chest, a heat building within her belly. One time . . . one more time she would kiss Vivian. She would ask . . . "Vivian."

"Bolt the door."

"Just a kiss."

"It's all I can handle."

"It's all I dare ask."

"Two foolish women, I'm thinkin'."

"Building pain."

"Storing memories, Elizabeth."

"Yes, that would be better."

Safe behind the locked door, Elizabeth sat on the

bed and leaned over Vivian, supporting herself with a hand on each side of Vivian's face.

"Storing memories," Vivian whispered.

Building pain, Elizabeth thought, and her lips closed on Vivian's.

Vivian's arms slipped around Elizabeth's neck as Elizabeth kissed her. Old excitement came flooding back as she took in Vivian's breath, the smell of her hair, the touch of her body through the gown.

She slid a hand beneath Vivian's shoulders, carefully holding her to her breast.

Their kiss lingered until they had searched one another's mouths, lips, tongues. Elizabeth kissed Vivian's ears and throat and the flesh exposed at the opened neck of her nightgown. She kissed her again, enraptured by the softness of Vivian's lips. She ran her hand over Vivian's breasts and down her ribcage, her hand rippling along her side.

Elizabeth could stand it no longer. With monumental will, she released her beloved Vivian.

Chapter 17

As Vivian and Elizabeth parted they heard a shout, followed by a loud pounding on the kitchen door.

"Something's wrong," Elizabeth said, hurrying toward the kitchen. Quickly she unlocked the door, and a breathless rider burst inside.

Vivian came slowly in from the bedroom. "Maudy Ellis, I declare . . ."

Closely following Maudy inside, Gerdy warned, "You go lay down, Vivian Blake. This doesn't concern you this time."

Maudy was a small woman dressed in a wide-brimmed hat, gray blouse, and brown split riding skirt. Elizabeth had met her last week when Maudy had ridden to Sheephaven to see how Vivian was. Her face was as white as a sheet as she said, "I need you, Elizabeth. Gerdy says you're available for a spell."

"She is," Gerdy stoutly confirmed. "Vivian's on the mend. I can handle things here."

"Elizabeth would be available for what?" Jonathan asked. He stood in the doorway, his face a mask of disbelief.

"He's available, too," Gerdy added, jerking a thumb his way.

Maudy said, "Ellen and Ed Slater's little girl is lost. Samuel and him's gone to get the crew from the H-Cross and the Swinging B. I'm on my way over to Dirk's ranch, next."

"It sounds like you already have plenty of help," Jonathan said.

Maudy glared at him. "We need more. And I heard Elizabeth ain't a quitter."

He bit back whatever he was thinking and asked, "How long will this take?"

"Till we find her," Maudy coldly answered.

"Elizabeth, come here." Jonathan led her outside and closed the door behind them. He guided her a short distance away, and said in a tightly controlled voice, "I've been patient with you, Elizabeth."

"I know that," she answered. She swung her arm as if to encompass the prairie. "But there's a little girl lost out there. We must help find her."

"Damn it, Elizabeth, come home. Now!" Sweat ran down his face into his eyes. "It's horrible out here. It's hot, empty . . . I *hate* it. And I hate it for you." He began to rub the bridge of his nose.

"After we find the girl," she flashed.

It was at this moment that Elizabeth fully realized how much she truly cared about these people. Their hopes and dreams and fears had become over the months, hers as well. She was no longer concerned with just Polly's, Andy's, or Vivian's well-being; she cared about everyone's with whom she came in contact. When had the change in her occurred? Remarkably, too, she had been asked by a near-stranger for help. Perhaps, when help was needed, there were no strangers in Montana.

Jonathan glared at her long and hard, his eyes never wavering from hers. He was as angry as Elizabeth had ever seen him. Wordlessly, they returned to the house.

She asked Maudy, "What will we need?"

"Grub, canteens, bedding," Maudy replied. "You might be out all night."

"And take my gun to signal with," Vivian added.

Elizabeth wore pants, a loose cotton shirt, boots, and a hat. She, Jonathan, and Al rode toward Slater's. Although she was uncomfortable, she noticed with satisfaction that after a half hour's ride she still did not hurt anywhere.

Her thoughts turned to the missing girl. Maudy had said that three-year-old Phoebe had wandered off early this morning while her mother had been out back of the soddy hanging up the wash.

Seeing Elizabeth's worried face, Al said in his big,

deep voice, "Relax, Elizabeth. We'll find her," quieting some of the fear within her.

It was hot, the kind of weather that could quickly kill a child, not to mention the ever-present danger of rattlesnakes lurking in the cooler draws where Phoebe might take shelter.

Jonathan dropped back, signaling Elizabeth to follow suit. "I want to talk to you," he said.

She was so tired of hearing that from him. "We've talked, Jonathan. Repeatedly."

He spoke gently to her, in control again. "I don't mean to be quarrelsome."

Softening, she replied, "I realize that." He was trying so hard. He took her hand, and they rode side by side.

"I need you for myself," he said, irritating her once more.

"Please, Jonathan. Not now." She spurred her horse, catching up with Al, leaving Jonathan to ride alone.

The Slater ranch was ten miles north of Vivian's spread, and steady riding brought them to the house sooner than they had hoped. Barking dogs announced their arrival.

Ellen Slater, in a faded dress, came out of the soddy. Peering around each side of her were a tow-headed boy and girl, their eyes as round as silver dollars. Mrs. Slater looked frantic and exhausted. Her brown hair hung in sweaty streaks around her face; her slate-gray eyes, smudged with dark circles, were filled with worry and fear. "Thank God you've come," she exclaimed. She wrung her hands.

Al asked, "What sections have been searched?"

She pointed to various parts of the land. "We've

been all around here and about a mile in that direction."

Three more riders rode up to the soddy. Ellen made brief introductions. Allen and Mary Smith rode together, and Floyd Barden had joined them about five miles back. Ellen repeated the range that had already been searched.

"We'll meet here at dark," Al said. "Whoever finds Phoebe first, fire your gun three times."

They broke into pairs, Elizabeth and Jonathan heading southeast, Al and Floyd to the north, and the Smiths working the west.

Elizabeth and Jonathan searched the draws, repeatedly calling out Phoebe's name, their throats sore from constant yelling, and both had to fight guzzling their water when they drank.

Now the sun was at its highest point, beating down on them; their clothes were saturated with sweat, the horses covered with froth. Elizabeth pulled off her hat and wiped her brow with her sleeve. Without the hat she felt as if her brains were baking inside her skull. How was little Phoebe to make it? she wondered desperately. She prayed the child would soon be found.

They stopped beneath a cottonwood for a few minutes to cool off. Jonathan held Elizabeth as she leaned heavily against him, his dark clothing emitting unpleasant heat. "It's nearly six," he said, looking at his pocketwatch. "We should work our way back."

She nodded, and they continued their search.

They checked any dip in the land, beneath bushes or in draws they might have missed. There were so many places a little girl could hide.

They were a mile from Slater's soddy when they heard the shots. Elizabeth wanted to beat Billy into a dead run, but she kept him to an even trot, and in a few minutes she slid exhaustedly from her saddle.

Ellen and Ed Slater sat before the sod house, Ellen tightly holding Phoebe wide-eyed and quiet in her lap, the boy and girl playing nearby. Ed held a cup of water in his hand, allowing the child just a small sip at a time.

The Smiths and Floyd Barden were already there, and others were riding in.

"Where was she?" Elizabeth asked as she slumped down beside them.

"A mile from here," Ed answered. "She'd followed her dog. They were sound asleep in a draw that had a wall washed out like a cave. It's a wonder we found her so soon."

"It's a blessing," Elizabeth said.

"No more damn dogs," Ellen snapped.

"Don't be foolish, Ellen," Ed replied softly. "You can't protect Phoebe that way."

Ellen closed her eyes. Tears slid down her cheeks. "I just get so frightened sometimes."

Ed knelt by her side. "It'll get better. I promise." He encircled his wife and daughter in his arms.

"It's time we got back," Al said.

Ed shook each rider's hand. "We can never thank you folks enough."

"Glad to help," Floyd said, speaking for all of them.

Elizabeth and Jonathan were soon back in the saddle.

* * * * *

227

They returned to Sheephaven to spend the night. Tomorrow, Elizabeth would go back to the Box R. Two days later she would be on a train with Jonathan, heading East. Everything here was finished. Vivian was getting better. The men and sheep were back out on the range. Summer was almost upon them. The circle was complete. Oddly, she felt left out.

"I'll miss you," she whispered to the land. She looked toward a mountain ridge where a pink glow flared and died as the sun dipped low on the horizon. It would be hot again tomorrow.

Elizabeth didn't expect to see a cool day until she reached New York where she would walk beneath the many tall maple and elm trees that surrounded her parents' home — her home.

She had been so busy she had not thought of the place in weeks. Of course, she would be just as busy when it came time to prepare for her wedding, and after the wedding itself there would be married life. She would have to look after servants and arrangements for dinners. Children would probably come along, taking up much of her time. There would be the nanny to attend to them during the day and evening hours, but she would see them mornings and afternoons.

"It all sounds so useless," she uttered.

"What does, darling?" Jonathan asked.

Elizabeth took off her hat and strung it across the saddle horn. "Nothing, Jonathan," she answered wearily. "Just — nothing."

"You're tired, dear," he said.
She certainly was.

Vivian was sound asleep, and Gerdy snored loudly from the parlor. Elizabeth stripped and quietly laid her clothes on the dresser, collapsing in her underwear on the cot.

Elizabeth heard Vivian stir. "Did you find Phoebe?" she whispered across the room.

"The Smiths found her," Elizabeth whispered back. "She's fine."

"Thank God."

"How are you doing?" Elizabeth asked.

"I feel good. I sat outside for a spell today. I get tired fast, but I'll be up soon, I'm thinkin'."

Vivian was quiet for so long that Elizabeth thought she had gone back to sleep until she said, "Come over here for a while." She sounded like her old self, giving orders in her low husky voice.

Elizabeth rose and slid in beside Vivian, slipping an arm beneath her.

"The doctor was here today," Vivian whispered. "He nearly dropped dead when he saw me. He doesn't think I'll get inflammation anymore."

Elizabeth hugged Vivian carefully. "You are such a courageous woman, Vivian."

"So are you."

"Don't be silly."

Vivian entwined her fingers in Elizabeth's hair.

"You don't know how much you've done since you've been here."

"Oh, I don't really think so."

"I know you don't, and that's the glory of it."

"Jonathan says I'm not the same little girl he once knew."

"He wants a little girl, does he?"

"He does."

"How foolish."

They laughed quietly together in the blackness of the house, their bodies in controlled convulsions until Vivian said, "I have to quit this carrying on. It's killing me." They forced themselves to be still.

"Will you sleep with me?" Vivian asked.

It wasn't the smart thing to do, but Elizabeth wanted to sleep with Vivian more than anything in the world.

"I'll stay," she said, and snuggled comfortably against her.

Chapter 18

Elizabeth groaned as she awoke, not sure where she was. There was a commotion going on just outside the house, the sound of a wagon rattling by, children loudly laughing, a dog barking. She peeled open her eyes and turned her head toward the bedroom door.

"Rise and shine, girl." Vivian spoke in a hearty voice. "Rise and shine." To Elizabeth's amazement, Vivian was fully dressed in a lovely green-checked calico dress.

Elizabeth moaned and rolled toward the wall. How

dare that woman feel better than she. And looking as pretty as a flower, too! She mumbled into the pillow, "What time is it?"

"Eight," came the cheery reply. "Get up. Folks are already arriving."

Elizabeth frowned and rolled over. "What folks?"

"Polly's here. Ellen's here with her kids and dogs. They're setting up tables over by the barbecue pits. Andy'll be along later. Donavans will be late."

"Why is everyone coming? Where's Jonathan?" Elizabeth sat up, brushing hair away from her face. She swung her feet to the floor.

"He and Henry left with the wagon before six this morning to get beef. Your aunt and uncle are throwing a going-away party for you two."

"They don't have to do that." Elizabeth pulled on fresh underwear and a blue cotton dress that Polly had apparently brought. She flung the covers across the bed. "How long have they been planning this?"

As soon as Elizabeth patted the pillows into place, Vivian lay down. "I don't know. A long time, I'd guess. Everybody's coming."

"Are you all right?"

"A little tired," Vivian said. "I walked out to the bunkhouse this morning."

"Don't overdo it," Elizabeth warned. She flopped onto the bed. "Lord, I'm tired."

"You're gonna be worse before this party's over."

"Why is it being held here?"

"I can't make it to the Box R."

"That was thoughtful of them, considering how Uncle Andy feels about sheepherders."

"And ain't that changed since winter? If it wasn't for sheep, a lot of those one-time cowmen would be

232

finished. I know four ranchmen in sheep this spring that were in cattle two months ago."

"I'd better go see Aunt Polly," Elizabeth said. At the sink she splashed cold water on her face, then attacked her hair with a brush and tied it into a bun.

"You look beautiful." Vivian had come into the kitchen.

Elizabeth blushed and smiled.

"Go see your aunt," Vivian said.

Elizabeth headed toward the pits beyond the bunkhouse, wishing Vivian didn't make her love so continuously obvious. It was too hard on Elizabeth, and it was hard on Vivian, too, if she would only admit it to herself.

At the pits, eight tables made of plank laid across oaken barrels were lined up end to end. Ellen Slater was busily laying out tablecloths and place settings. Polly shoveled fuel into the pits. Heartily, she greeted Elizabeth.

"Good morning, Aunt Polly." Elizabeth hugged her and said to Ellen, "How's Phoebe today?"

"Oh, she's a fit as a fiddle, thanks to good folks like you pitching in," Ellen answered happily. "My husband and I can't imagine an Eastern woman wiling to do what you did, Elizabeth."

"Jonathan's from the East, and he helped," Elizabeth reminded her. "Mary Smith helped too."

"Jonathan's a man, and Mary's been here for years. They're expected to help."

"Well, I'm here too, Ellen, and I should be expected to, as well."

Polly laid aside her shovel and came over to Elizabeth, gripping her niece's shoulders. She shook her head from side to side. "My goodness. I'm so proud of you, Elizabeth. I could just bust my buttons."

"Oh, Aunt Polly, stop."

"Your father would throw a fit if he could see you now. Tan as leather, tough as rawhide."

"He'll see me soon enough, Aunt Polly." Elizabeth picked up a stack of plates and began to lay them out.

"When do you leave?" Ellen asked. She snapped a checkered oilcloth in the air and whipped it over a table.

"We were going today," Elizabeth answered. "But I see you folks have other plans. Frankly I'm glad. I'm not anxious to leave."

"We'll hate to see you go," Polly said.

Elizabeth couldn't have agreed with her more.

At ten o'clock, Henry and Jonathan arrived with two half-carcasses of beef wrapped in burlap. Jonathan had finally shed his suit for a red flannel shirt and rough woolen pants tucked into high-heeled boots. Elizabeth guessed the clothing belonged to Al, the only man around matching Jonathan's large size. Henry skewered the meat, and he and Jonathan hung it over the glowing coals.

Henry left immediately for the range, saying that either he or Al would be back tonight.

"Are you finished here?" Jonathan asked, gesturing to the tables.

Elizabeth nodded.

"Go relax, you two," Polly insisted, pushing them

away from the area. "Take a walk. Ellen and I will turn the meat."

"I could help, Aunt Polly," Elizabeth offered.

Polly slapped her smartly on the rump. "Git!"

Jonathan took her by the arm and leaned close to her. Grinning, he said, "You certainly like to pitch in, don't you?"

"I like to feel useful."

"You'll be very useful when we return home."

"Yes, I suppose I will be."

"Of course you will be," he said. "How can you not?" He smiled brilliantly and placed his arm across her shoulders.

She bent to pick a blade of grass to escape the feeling of ownership his contact radiated. "I think it's rather nice of Aunt Polly and Uncle Andy to see us off this way," she said. "I've made some good friends. I welcome the opportunity to say goodbye to them. Try to enjoy yourself today, Jonathan. We don't have to do anything but have fun. And tomorrow we'll be gone. Come on. I'd like to see how Vivian is doing." She linked her arm through his.

"Elizabeth," he groaned.

Impatiently, she said, "I'll only be a minute."

He waited at the bedroom door. Vivian was asleep, but she opened her eyes as Elizabeth approached the bed.

"How are you feeling?" Elizabeth asked. Had they been alone, she would have brushed the damp strands of hair away from Vivian's face and cooled her skin with a wet cloth.

"I'm fine," Vivian replied. She saw Jonathan standing in the doorway. "You look like a regular hand, Mr. Stanton. Come in here where I can get a better look at you."

Jonathan came forward for her inspection.

"He'd make a hell of a good-looking sheepherder, wouldn't he?"

Elizabeth smiled. "I think so."

"If you'll excuse us," Jonathan said. Again, he waited by the door.

It surprised Elizabeth to see him pinching the bridge of his nose.

Vivian gazed intently into Elizabeth's eyes. "Enjoy yourselves," she said. "Take care of her, Mr. Stanton. She's a regular gal."

By six, Sheephaven bustled with life. Men and women chatted and laughed in groups. Children and dogs ran everywhere. With homes so widely scattered, where had so many people come from, Elizabeth wondered.

She introduced Jonathan to everyone she knew, and Polly and Andy introduced them to still others. Elizabeth could not remember all the names.

John Abernathy, from over on the Mussellshell River, had hauled in a load of wide-cut floor planks. "I ain't laying the floor till tomorrow, folks. Let's use 'em. Boys, get ready to grab yer women!"

There was a rousing shout as the men quickly emptied the wagon, laying the planks side by side. In minutes, the sound of a fiddle split the air, and a deep voice from the thinnest man Elizabeth had ever seen called to the square-dancing couples.

Calico dresses trimmed with ruffles whirled in a

236

cascade of color as men and boys in denim and overalls swung their ladies around the floor. Hands clapped in rhythm and people hummed along.

Elizabeth danced numerous times, her partners laughing heartily at her mistakes. She laughed right along with them, doubling over with hysterics as she struggled to keep up the demanding pace.

She and Jonathan danced a few round dances, but he refused to try square dancing. "How about a Virginia Reel?" he suggested.

The caller heard him and shouted, "Virginia Reel. Grab your partners." Jonathan danced with fluid grace, raising cheers of approval and encouragement.

Elizabeth finally claimed exhaustion. "Come on, Jonathan. Let's eat."

The tables were laden with vegetables, boiled and baked potatoes, fruit pies, cookies, cakes, roasted chicken, and thick slabs of beef. They heaped their plates high and sat down to enjoy their meal.

Hilda Donavan came over, little Mark asleep in her arms.

"Join us, Hilda," Elizabeth invited, patting the bench beside her.

"Marcus and me want to tell you how pleased we were that you helped us." She shifted Mark in her lap and shyly added, "You pulled us through."

"Nonsense, Hilda. Frankly, I was afraid I wouldn't know how to do anything. At least now I can make a decent stew."

"And bake biscuits. You tried her biscuits yet, Mr. Stanton?"

"No, I haven't. I didn't realize she was an accomplished cook."

"Why, Mr. Stanton! All women are accomplished cooks."

"Of course," he answered.

Elizabeth hid a smile behind her hand and watched Jonathan's face turn red.

Marcus joined them, shaking Jonathan's hand and smiling at Elizabeth. "Fine woman, Mr. Stanton. Fine woman." He and Hilda filled their plates. Mark awoke and demanded his share of the food. Hilda mashed potatoes and fed him bites.

Vivian and Henry arrived, Vivian resting heavily against his arm. Henry carefully helped Vivian onto the bench opposite Elizabeth and Jonathan.

A flicker of trepidation crossed Jonathan's face. "Up and about are we, Vivian?"

Elizabeth frowned, nudging him sharply.

"Just wanted to say goodbye, Missy," Henry said. "Al says so, too." He sat next to Vivian, fumbling with his string tie. He cleared his throat and then carefully placed two small gifts wrapped in brown paper and narrow red ribbon before Elizabeth.

"Why, Henry. You shouldn't have."

"They're from me and Al. This here one's from Al. He says you're to open his before I leave."

"Go on, Elizabeth, open it," Vivian encouraged.

Elizabeth drew a lantern close and unwrapped the package. Inside was a small, flat piece of wood, sanded as smooth as glass and delicately inscribed with black ink:

> A little bummer left alone,
> Momma's heart as dead as stone,
> Cared for by kind, loving hands,
> Now Bummer lives on buffalo grass.

"Bummer," she whispered.

"What's it mean?" Jonathan asked her.

"I took care of the motherless lambs this spring. Henry gave me the first baby for my very own. How I'll miss that little lamb."

"Al made the poem up hisself, Missy."

She smiled tearfully at the old shepherd. "It's a very beautiful poem, Henry. Please tell him I said so."

She opened Henry's gift and looked at it in awe. Carved from cottonwood and blackened with charcoal, a miniature lamb seemed to spring to life in her hand, so perfect was it in detail. Little ringlets of wool covered the body. Fine lines delineated the wool's texture. She ran her hands over the statue as if to feel Bummer's soft coat once again. "I had no idea you were so gifted, Henry."

Obviously pleased, he said, "It's so you don't forget you got a darn good sheep out here, Missy, an' you always will have."

"I could never forget Bummer, Henry. Not in a million years." She moved to the opposite side of the table and sat beside him. "You and Al have been so kind."

"You done good for us, Missy."

She hugged the old sheepherder. He smelled familiarly of sweat, sheep, and tobacco. Awkwardly, he patted her shoulder.

They all sat and talked for some time, the men discussing the terrible weather and the thousands of cattle lost and ranches that had failed. The women talked of children and cooking and bedbugs that could infest a soddy in a day if you as much as let one of the miserable creatures inside. It was earthy, homey

239

talk, the Montanans' soft accents falling pleasantly on Elizabeth's ears.

As darkness fell, the night grew comfortably cool. "Well," Jonathan announced, "I think Elizabeth and I will take a walk."

"It's time I got back, too," Vivian said. "Gerdy's probably already at the house wondering where I am." Henry stood to help her.

Elizabeth's longing to be the one who helped Vivian was nearly palpable. She wished she could have spent more time with Vivian this final day at Sheephaven. It took all her effort to walk away with Jonathan.

Dancers still whirled on the floor; dozens of lanterns cast their golden glow across the floor. A couple of people beckoned her to join them.

"Later!" she called out, waving to them.

She felt the strong pull of these people who had made her so much a part of their lives. They made her want to belong. And that wasn't all of it. She shook her head.

Jonathan gave her arm a slight tug, drawing her attention back to him. Frowning, he asked, "Are you all right?"

"I'm fine," she said.

As they walked, bright rays cast by the moon pushed deep shadows ahead of them. She was reminded of another moonlit walk late last fall when, arm in arm, she and Vivian had strolled the prairie.

She swallowed hard. An idea leaped into her mind. Did she dare suggest the thought to Jonathan? Her heart beat in thick, rapid rhythm, but as calmly as possible she said, "Jonathan, let's not go back to New

York." As she spoke the words, she knew with dead certainty she could never leave Montana.

He spoke harshly. "Don't talk stupidly. Your visit is over."

"I'm not talking about a visit. I'm talking about a permanent move. I'm asking if you would consider living here. There's so much we can do. And it would count for something."

He loomed over her. "What I do in New York counts. Your being a wife and mother would certainly count."

"I could be a wife and mother here — and do more. I could help in ways I never dreamed possible back home."

"You're no more needed here than a rich man needs a tattered coat. I want you to stop talking like a woman gone berserk. You're beginning to worry me considerably." There was confusion and pain in his eyes.

She moved away from him. "These people need me."

He reached out and snatched her to his breast. "*I* need you!" Forcefully, he turned her face toward the animated dancers, their laughter floating out over the plains. "They don't need you. Look at them." She tried to pull away, but he held her jaw in an iron grip. "*Look* at them," he insisted. "There isn't one thing wrong with any one of them. There is nothing that needs fixing. There is nothing for you to *do!*"

She wrenched away from his hand. "But there will be. Oh, not right now. Not right this minute, but tomorrow, or next week, or next month there may be."

His face was inches from hers. "They have each other. They did before you came. They will long after you've gone."

She felt her blood boil. "I want them to have me, too."

His voice trembled as he spoke. "And how are we to live, to make out? There's no work for me here."

"We have Bummer. She's the beginning of something."

"One sheep. Good Lord, Elizabeth!"

"Back home I am a pampered woman. Here — I count. As a helpmate, not as an ornament."

"You're an outsider."

"I couldn't tell that tonight. Nor have I been able to for a long time. I've only just begun to realize that fact."

An animal-like voice came from deep within him, and his face became twisted and ugly. He grabbed her by the arm and began dragging her toward the horses and wagons. "We're leaving. Now!"

"Stop, Jonathan. Don't *do* this. I . . . love you." She tried to wrest herself from his grasp.

He propelled her toward the wagon, nearly carrying her. Through gritted teeth, he said, "I love you, Elizabeth."

In a rage, she fought him, kicking him and slapping at his arms and face. "Jonathan, you've gone mad. *Stop!* You're hurting me." Even now, she kept her angry voice low so that their shameful struggle could not be heard.

They reached his buggy, and he tried without success to force her onto the seat. Tears streamed down her face as she clung desperately to the wheel, her hands slowly slipping from the rim as he pulled her away.

"Going for a drive, folks?" Andy appeared out of the darkness, his voice questioning, searching, dangerously low.

"Uncle Andy," Elizabeth gasped. Hastily, she wiped away her tears.

Jonathan relaxed his grip on her, saying accusingly, "She's talking about living here. But I'm taking her back to New York."

"That so? Right now, I take it."

"Immediately."

"Doesn't look as though she wants to leave tonight, Jonathan."

With shaking hands, Elizabeth smoothed her hair and dress. She trembled from head to toe, her voice unsteady, her knees weak. "I don't want to leave at all, Uncle Andy."

Andy stood threateningly before Jonathan. "Don't you think you ought to let it go at that, Mr. Stanton? See how things look in the morning."

Elizabeth moved between them, fearing these men would start fighting. She put a hand on the arm of each, feeling the tension ripple beneath their sleeves.

Other men had drifted over, attracted by the angry voices. They shifted uneasily from one foot to the other. Elizabeth forced herself to smile. "Everything is all right, gentlemen. Please leave. Everything is fine." Reluctantly, they backed away, drifting toward the dance floor. She turned to her uncle. "I'll be fine, Uncle Andy. I wish you would go, too."

"You're sure, Elizabeth?" Andy still stood before

Jonathan, having to look up at the taller man, but not backing down an inch.

"I'm sure, Uncle Andy." She kissed him reassuringly on the cheek. "I'll be all right."

He left, glancing back frequently.

Alone again, Jonathan grabbed Elizabeth's hand. "You frighten me, darling. I love you. I can't live without you. I've tried so hard for you, tried to be a good sport about being here. Come, let's just get into the buggy and leave. We can rest at the Box R tonight. Tomorrow we can get an early start. Begin over —"

"Nothing has changed, Jonathan," she answered firmly. "I'm not going with you. Not tonight. Not tomorrow. Not ever."

"But you love me. You told me so not moments ago." His voice cracked with pain. "Is it because I was so rough? I'm sorry. I'm very sorry." She could feel his chest heaving. "Would you have felt useless if you had never come out here? Would never having traveled kept you the same?"

"I would have remained the same woman you knew. But I would have been discontent and never have known why. Now I know why."

Watching Henry with Vivian earlier this evening had triggered Elizabeth's rebellion. She was the one, the *only* one who should have been helping Vivian. Elizabeth knew it with as much certainty as she knew the sun would rise to bake the earth tomorrow.

"Then *why?*" he cried.

But she did not answer.

He said, "There are charities you could work for."

"No, Jonathan. The women sit and chat, hardly

making a dent in what really needs to be done. It's nothing but a show for most of those who go."

"Make it more than that. You could do it."

"No."

"Oh, God, Elizabeth, *don't stay.*" He broke down in tears and turned away from her.

"You'll find another." She felt so cold saying it. So remote. She felt as if she did not love him, had not loved him for a long time.

She moved away from him and stood stock still, but he came to her and crushed her again to his breast. "I've lost you. *Lost* you."

Fiercely, brutally, he kissed her. He threw back his head, crying out at the sky. "*Damn* Montana!"

"Go back to New York in the morning, Jonathan." She spoke softly. "You belong there as surely as I belong here."

"Why? Why be that strong?"

"Because I am that strong."

"You say you love me, and yet you don't even look as though you would regret my going."

"Vivian needs me." To hell with it. She would say all of it.

"*Vivian* needs you? What the hell do you mean Vivian needs you? *I* need you. I've told you a thousand times."

"I need her," she answered simply. And that was the truth of it.

His body rippled as if in shock. "*You're crazy!*" he hissed. He thrust her aside and flung himself onto the buggy. "I'll *never* be back. You can count on that! To have wasted my time on you — *damn* you!" Bitter disappointment poured from his eyes. Cursing wildly, he snapped the reins against the horse's flanks and drove swiftly into the darkness.

When she could no longer see him, she sank wearily to the ground.

"Elizabeth." Andy appeared at her side.

"Uncle Andy . . ."

"I've been nearby." He squatted down beside her. "You all right?"

She nodded without speaking.

"You're making a big mistake, Elizabeth."

"Aunt Polly, my parents . . ."

"You'll have to take your licks alone. In the meantime, I'd better follow after Jonathan. Talk some reason into him so's he'll wait until morning at least in case he's thinking of leaving tonight." He hugged her and kissed the top of her head and then walked away, the grass muting his steps.

Elizabeth got shakily to her feet and took several deep breaths to calm herself. She looked to where Jonathan had disappeared, and a wave of peace washed over her.

She walked slowly toward the house, gaining speed until she was running full force. She wasn't afraid of stepping on a snake, or of hearing the coyote's howl that broke out over the prairie, or the nearby mournful staccato answer from another coyote. She wasn't afraid of anything this land threw at her: its terrible cold winters; its treeless, monstrous space; the uncertainty that each day could bring — none of it did she fear.

She smelled the aroma of grass crushed beneath her feet, heard a couple laugh off to her right, saw the silhouette of a tiny animal scamper by in the moonlight, rushing to get out of her path. She figured Andy would tell people easily enough what had happened to her and Jonathan. Tomorrow she would deal with the issue. But right now she knew where she wanted to be.

She stopped short at the door and waited until she breathed normally again. Quietly, she entered the house. In the bedroom, she didn't bother to light a lantern. She knew her way around well enough. She dropped her dress over a chair and then walked over to the bed. Vivian shifted as she climbed in, the mattress making a wonderfully familiar rustling sound.

"Vivian," Elizabeth whispered. She felt Vivian's arm slide across her chest. "Vivian," she whispered again. "I have something I must tell you."

"In the morning," Vivian answered sleepily, resting her cheek against Elizabeth's.

"It's important, Vivian. I need to tell you — that I have a . . . a . . . a Montana heart," she blurted.

Vivian slowly sat up, looking down at Elizabeth in the pale light of the room. "A Montana heart?" she asked doubtfully. "You've got a Montana heart?"

"Yes!"

"You mean you'll be staying for a little while longer, is that what you're saying?"

"For a long time, Vivian. For a very long time."

Vivian fell backward onto her pillow. Elizabeth could see the gleam of her teeth as she smiled wide. She shouted joyously, "Hey, Gerdy! Elizabeth's got a Montana heart! That makes her blind stubborn and a fool to boot! I told her that last summer."

"Shhh," Elizabeth said, clamping her hand over Vivian's mouth.

They froze and listened. From the parlor, came a loud undignified snore.

They threw back their heads and laughed, and then drew together and kissed long and deep.

Vivian whispered, "Ah, Elizabeth Reynolds, I love you."

"I love you, my wild sheepherder," Elizabeth answered.

They kissed again. "Tomorrow we'll send Gerdy packing."

"First thing," Elizabeth promptly agreed.

They snuggled tightly together, making contented little noises, and fell into peaceful slumber.

A few of the publications of
THE NAIAD PRESS, INC.
P.O. Box 10543 ● Tallahassee, Florida 32302
Phone (904) 539-5965
Mail orders welcome. Please include 15% postage.

DEATH DOWN UNDER by Claire McNab. 240 pp. 3rd Det.
Insp. Carol Ashton mystery.　　　　ISBN 0-941483-39-8　　$8.95

MONTANA FEATHERS by Penny Hayes. 256 pp. Vivian and
Elizabeth find love in frontier Montana.　ISBN 0-941483-61-4　　8.95

CHESAPEAKE PROJECT by Phyllis Horn. 304 pp. Jessie &
Meredith in perilous adventure.　　ISBN 0-941483-58-4　　8.95

LIFESTYLES by Jackie Calhoun. 224 pp. Contemporary Lesbian
lives and loves.　　　　　　　　ISBN 0-941483-57-6　　8.95

VIRAGO by Karen Marie Christa Minns. 208 pp. Darsen has
chosen Ginny.　　　　　　　　　ISBN 0-941483-56-8　　8.95

WILDERNESS TREK by Dorothy Tell. 192 pp. Six women on
vacation learning "new" skills.　　ISBN 0-941483-60-6　　8.95

MURDER BY THE BOOK by Pat Welch. 256 pp. A Helen
Black Mystery. First in a series.　　ISBN 0-941483-59-2　　8.95

BERRIGAN by Vicki P. McConnell. 176 pp. Youthful Lesbian–
romantic, idealistic Berrigan.　　　ISBN 0-941483-55-X　　8.95

LESBIANS IN GERMANY by Lillian Faderman & B. Eriksson.
128 pp. Fiction, poetry, essays.　　ISBN 0-941483-62-2　　8.95

THE BEVERLY MALIBU by Katherine V. Forrest. 288 pp. A
Kate Delafield Mystery. 3rd in a series.　ISBN 0-941483-47-9　　16.95

THERE'S SOMETHING I'VE BEEN MEANING TO TELL
YOU Ed. by Loralee MacPike. 288 pp. Gay men and lesbians
coming out to their children.　　　ISBN 0-941483-44-4　　9.95
　　　　　　　　　　　　　　　ISBN 0-941483-54-1　　16.95

LIFTING BELLY by Gertrude Stein. Ed. by Rebecca Mark. 104
pp. Erotic poetry.　　　　　　　ISBN 0-941483-51-7　　8.95
　　　　　　　　　　　　　　　ISBN 0-941483-53-3　　14.95

ROSE PENSKI by Roz Perry. 192 pp. Adult lovers in a long-term
relationship.　　　　　　　　　ISBN 0-941483-37-1　　8.95

AFTER THE FIRE by Jane Rule. 256 pp. Warm, human novel
by this incomparable author.　　　ISBN 0-941483-45-2　　8.95

SUE SLATE, PRIVATE EYE by Lee Lynch. 176 pp. The gay
folk of Peacock Alley are *all* cats.　ISBN 0-941483-52-5　　8.95

CHRIS by Randy Salem. 224 pp. Golden oldie. Handsome Chris
and her adventures.　　　　　　ISBN 0-941483-42-8　　8.95

THREE WOMEN by March Hastings. 232 pp. Golden oldie. A
triangle among wealthy sophisticates.　ISBN 0-941483-43-6　　8.95

RICE AND BEANS by Valeria Taylor. 232 pp. Love and
romance on poverty row.   ISBN 0-941483-41-X   8.95

PLEASURES by Robbi Sommers. 204 pp. Unprecedented
eroticism.   ISBN 0-941483-49-5   8.95

EDGEWISE by Camarin Grae. 372 pp. Spellbinding
adventure.   ISBN 0-941483-19-3   9.95

FATAL REUNION by Claire McNab. 216 pp. 2nd Det. Inspec.
Carol Ashton mystery.   ISBN 0-941483-40-1   8.95

KEEP TO ME STRANGER by Sarah Aldridge. 372 pp. Romance
set in a department store dynasty.   ISBN 0-941483-38-X   9.95

HEARTSCAPE by Sue Gambill. 204 pp. American lesbian in
Portugal.   ISBN 0-941483-33-9   8.95

IN THE BLOOD by Lauren Wright Douglas. 252 pp. Lesbian
science fiction adventure fantasy   ISBN 0-941483-22-3   8.95

THE BEE'S KISS by Shirley Verel. 216 pp. Delicate, delicious
romance.   ISBN 0-941483-36-3   8.95

RAGING MOTHER MOUNTAIN by Pat Emmerson. 264 pp.
Furosa Firechild's adventures in Wonderland. ISBN 0-941483-35-5   8.95

IN EVERY PORT by Karin Kallmaker. 228 pp. Jessica's sexy,
adventuresome travels.   ISBN 0-941483-37-7   8.95

OF LOVE AND GLORY by Evelyn Kennedy. 192 pp. Exciting
WWII romance.   ISBN 0-941483-32-0   8.95

CLICKING STONES by Nancy Tyler Glenn. 288 pp. Love
transcending time.   ISBN 0-941483-31-2   8.95

SURVIVING SISTERS by Gail Pass. 252 pp. Powerful love
story.   ISBN 0-941483-16-9   8.95

SOUTH OF THE LINE by Catherine Ennis. 216 pp. Civil War
adventure.   ISBN 0-941483-29-0   8.95

WOMAN PLUS WOMAN by Dolores Klaich. 300 pp. Supurb
Lesbian overview.   ISBN 0-941483-28-2   9.95

SLOW DANCING AT MISS POLLY'S by Sheila Ortiz Taylor.
96 pp. Lesbian Poetry   ISBN 0-941483-30-4   7.95

DOUBLE DAUGHTER by Vicki P. McConnell. 216 pp. A Nyla
Wade Mystery, third in the series.   ISBN 0-941483-26-6   8.95

These are just a few of the many Naiad Press titles — we are the oldest and
largest lesbian/feminist publishing company in the world. Please request a
complete catalog. We offer personal service; we encourage and welcome
direct mail orders from individuals who have limited access to bookstores
carrying our publications.